GARDENS OF NIGHT
by GREG F. GIFUNE
author of
DEEP NIGHT
and
THE BLEEDING SEASON

Recovering from an unthinkably violent trauma, Marcus Banyon comes to perceive a *different* reality. Have his eyes been opened to forces long hidden from the rest of humanity, or has he suffered a psychotic break as his doctors suggest? As he retreats to an isolated chalet with his also-recovering wife and his oldest friend, Marc's visions lead them to an ancient mythology steeped in mystery and terror ... and to a trio of sinister beings who hold the fate of the world in their hands.

GARDENS OF NIGHT

Greg F. Gifune

UNINVITED BOOKS

This book is a work of fiction. Names, characters, places and incidents are products of the author's imagination or are used fictiously. Any resemblance to actual events or to persons, living or dead, is entirely coincidental.

Copyright © 2010 by Greg F. Gifune

All rights reserved, including the right to reproduce this book or portions thereof in any form whatsoever. For information contact Editor@UninvitedBooks.com or visit www.UninvitedBooks.com.

Cover artwork by Chas Hendricksen

Author photo by Carol Gifune

Manufactured in the United States

First Uninvited Books paperback edition November 2010

ISBN: 978-0-9830457-1-7

For LeShelle Woodard

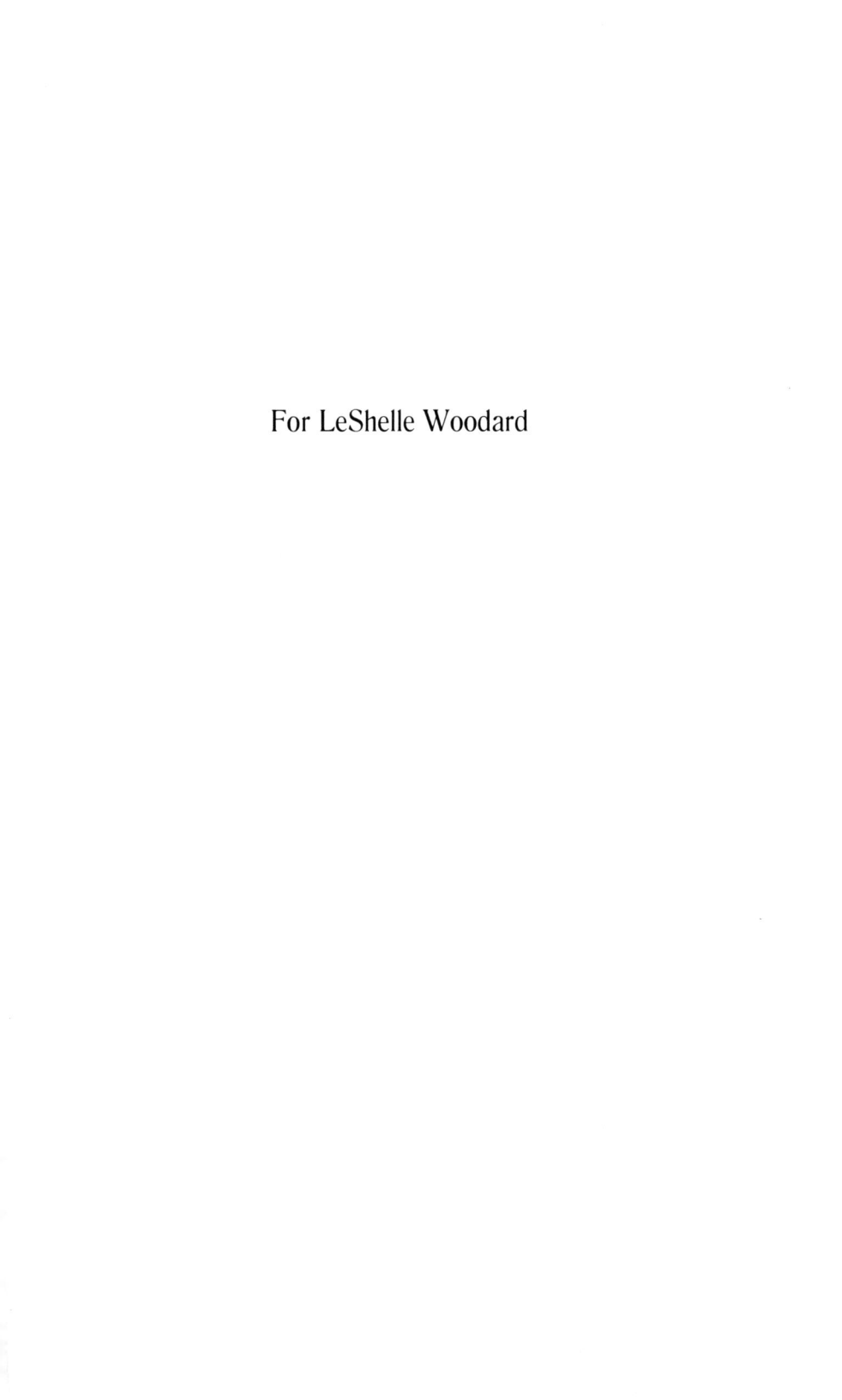

Also by Greg F. Gifune

The Living and the Dead
Long After Dark
Kingdom of Shadows
Catching Hell
Children of Chaos
Judas Goat
Saying Uncle
Dominion
A View from the Lake
Blood in Electric Blue
Deep Night
The Bleeding Season
Heretics
Down to Sleep
Drago Descending
Night Work

"The world of men is dreaming, it has gone mad in its sleep, and a snake is strangling it, but it can't wake up."
~ D. H. Lawrence

PROLOGUE

It moves through the tall grass like a shadow, glimpses of its bushy tail the only indication the creature is actual rather than a trick of light and imagination. At the edge of the field, the fox hesitates, cocks his head and smells the air. A cold late October breeze drifts down from the summit of a distant hill, across the open field then filters through the tall grass beyond, causing the stalks to sway back and forth like countless summoning fingers. Though dusk has only just arrived, the dense forest on the far side has already fallen dark. Most of the leaves have turned a brilliant yellow, brown and orange, but soon—very soon—they will fall dead and winter will set in. For now, only night comes. And that's enough. It sneaks about like the wind, stirring all that resides within it, but despite the shift of light and dark, time seems to have ground to a stop here, and it is eerily quiet.

The fox senses this peculiar change in the air but remains still, his eyes trained on an enormous tree atop the hill. Ancient, with a thick trunk and long gnarled branches that reach toward the ashen sky like tendrils, the tree, barren and blackened as if horribly burned years ago, stands alone on the horizon, a sentry watching over all that lies beyond it.

The wells… the farmhouse… the sisters…

The past… the present… the future…

Bounding with as much power as grace, the fox darts across the field, stealthily ascends the hill then pulls up just short of the massive tree.

Four deer watch the fox from the base of the tree, their heads raised and turned. His presence is enough to startle them, and the deer sprint away across the opposite field to the rear of the farmhouse below. A rush of wind stirs in their wake as they instinctively cut a wide swath around the old barn before disappearing into the woods.

The fox's eyes shift to the three quaint wooden wells with draw buckets not far from the tree.

But something else distracts him.

Below, a dull yellow light fills one of the farmhouse windows.

They're awake.

Night falls harder, faster.

A large gray serpent slithers through the tree above and silently coils around a nearby branch. Its forked tongue flickers, black liquid eyes lifeless yet mocking.

The front door to the aged farmhouse opens with a noisy creak, and the sound echoes up along the hillside. A shadow figure emerges, its body covered from head to toe in what appears to be a dark shroud of some kind. Two more follow in single file, each holding a burning candle as they move across the farm toward the hill. The shrouds brush the ground and conceal their feet, but the three figures hold such upright postures and rigid strides that the fox cannot be sure if they're walking or gliding, floating just above the earth.

Suddenly, the fox smells something.

Danger.

He turns and runs back in the direction from which he came, not stopping or even slowing until he reaches the forest. Once within the boundary of trees he comes to a gradual halt and looks back.

In the distance, three women stand watching from the top of the hill.

But surely they can't see him from such a distance. Can they?

As he slips away beneath the cover of darkness, all the fox knows for sure is that on this strange and cold October night he is no longer the predator here.

They are.

"In the dreamer's dream, the dreamed one awoke."
~ Jorge Luis Borges

One

Shine...
 He must remember that he sees things differently now, even when he's asleep. Dreams, his sanctuary, come easily. They are all that remains to protect him from the darkness, the emptiness. His dreams have always been vivid, though of late they've become more so, since the pills, the tiny tablets designed to relax and center him, to make him feel less anxious and depressed. They work, but who knows what they're doing to him long-term? The doctors claim they're perfectly safe, but safety is a myth.
 Sounds of sleep, of magic, drift away, leaving him in uncertain silence. From his slumped position on the edge of the bed, Marcus Banyon peers down at the small plastic bottle in his hand, the childproof cap and prescription sticker. More shackles, more chains. But exactly what are they shackling him *to*? He cannot be certain. Not yet.
 Marc twists free the cap, drops a pill into his palm then grabs a bottle of water from the nightstand. Before he can further analyze the situation, he pops the tablet into his mouth and washes it down.
 "Are you all right?"
 Rather than turn toward the voice, he stares at the floor.
 "If I never hear that question again it'll be too soon."

"I'm sorry," she says.

"Don't be."

"*How are you?* Is that better?"

Marc gives a listless nod.

She remains in the doorway. Something prevents her from crossing fully into the room. The shades in the bedroom are drawn, but the light behind her leaves her in silhouette and hints at either dusk or dawn. It hardly matters which. "Are you sure you're up for this?" Brooke asks. "We don't *have* to go."

"Spaulding went to a lot of trouble to set this up, we can't disappoint him."

"It's not about disappointing Spaulding. It's about what's best for you."

"And you."

"I think it might be good for everyone."

He wishes she sounded more convincing.

"Sometimes a change of scenery can be a really positive thing. Even the doctor said it might be good to get away somewhere quiet and—"

"It's all right," he assures her. "It's fine."

"I'm just saying if you'd rather stay home and rest here—or if you think that's best—it's not a big deal."

"Brooke," he says, hoping the sound of her name will quiet her, "we've already had this conversation. It's fine. I'm fine. We'll go and it'll be great."

"You're sure?"

He never answers.

"I checked on you earlier," she eventually says. "You were dreaming. It looked like you were concentrating on something."

He doesn't reply for a long while. "Have you ever heard whale songs?"

"Yes. Yes, of course."

"That's what I hear when I dream now. Sometimes I even hear traces of them in that moment when I first come awake, these beautiful ethereal sounds."

She fidgets about uncomfortably. "I thought maybe you were dreaming about, you know, what happened."

"I only dream about that when I'm awake." He runs a hand through his thinning hair. It's neither cold nor warm in the bedroom, but his scalp is damp with perspiration. "When I sleep, I dream of other things. I hear the whales."

"Are the whales talking to you, Marc?"

"They must be. Why else would I hear them?"

"What do they say?"

"I think they're asking for deliverance."

"From what?"

"Sadness. Pain."

Brooke clears her throat awkwardly. "They're in pain?"

"Everything alive is in pain."

"And they think you can help them?"

He knows she's only pretending, playing along with what she perceives as his inadequacies and impairment, but he explains as best he can anyway. These are new thoughts in his head, fresh mysteries he's still sifting through himself. "We have the power but we hide instead. We hide in the pain until we can't take another second of it."

She hugs herself as if overtaken by a sudden chill. "And then?"

"We use it like a mallet to smash each other to pieces."

"Why?" Brooke angles her head to the side in an attempt to see beyond him to the shadows nesting in the far corner. "Why whale songs?"

"I think it might be because they're so hard to ignore once you've heard them. If someone or something wanted to communicate, to tell us something important, wouldn't they use something universally compelling? There's something about them, something spiritually primal that speaks to us even if we're not listening or don't understand. You can feel it, there's something more there, something deeper, something haunting and frightening, yet beautiful, peaceful. Sometimes their cries sound almost human. And once we hear those songs they're always with us. We never forget them." He finally raises his head and looks at her. He wishes he could see her face, but it remains cloaked in shadow. "How do you forget the voice of God?" Though he smiles, there are tears in his eyes. "How do you forget when it's so helpless?"

※

Colorful foliage decorates the trees on either side of the highway. Marc watches it rush past the car window in a smeared blur, varied shades of gold and red, yellow and brown. He wonders how—and why—such beauty can precede death. It's a troubling realization, and yet strangely soothing to know that even at the end, there is splendor.

He sits alone in the backseat. Brooke and Spaulding are up front. Spaulding drives, it's his car after all—a rental actually, a midsize sedan he had waiting for him at Logan Airport when he flew in from Chicago—but Marc can't help thinking he and Brooke are the couple, they should be sitting together, not apart. And if they're to be apart, shouldn't Marc be the one in the front seat with Spaulding? These thoughts puzzle him; leave him confused as to why they're even coursing through his head. They're petty and childish, but for some reason he cannot ignore them. It reminds him of early on in their relationship, when Spaulding and Brooke were the couple and he was the third wheel, the clumsy friend along for the ride. He'd felt awkward then, but that was years ago, they'd still been teenagers. Now he feels something else. The more he thinks about it, focuses on it, and watches them chatting and interacting, these two people he has known longer than anyone else—his wife and his oldest friend—the foolish thoughts subside and are replaced with ones more benign. No, it's not semantics that bother him, nor the often complicated history they share, nor the knowledge that before Brooke was his wife she was Spaulding's girlfriend. Those are things familiar and known to them all, things that have evolved and grown with them as people, as friends, as a trio over the course of many years. Rather, the true source of his agitation is the conversation he overheard prior to leaving the house. He knows in his heart they meant well, but the conspiratorial tone of their discussion stays with him, gnaws at him even now, an hour or more later.

Finally, the tangle of thoughts in his mind congeal into something decipherable, and he remembers lying awake, the bedroom door ajar as he listened to them talk in the nearby kitchen.

"How's he been?"

"About the same, he has good days and bad."

"And his doctor's OK with us going away for a while?"

"As long as Marc's comfortable with the idea she thinks it has the potential to be very cathartic."

"Well, he's obviously come a long way. At least he's home."

"Yeah, it's just..."

"Tell me."

"It's like at times he's someone else. He has these disjointed thoughts when he's awake, and he hears strange things in his sleep."

"Like what?"

"Animals and spirits – the universe – communicating with him through his dreams or – I don't know – I don't understand any of it. It's like his senses have heightened or sharpened or something. He seems much more susceptible to everything around him."

"So are we talking delusions or some sort of avoidance?"

"I don't know. Even the doctors aren't sure. But Marc believes it."

"That may be all that matters."

"That night changed him, Spaulding. It changed us both."

"How could it not? You guys have been through hell. It's going to take time."

"But much as Marc seems to want to, he hasn't been able to dig his way out. I've managed to but he can't."

"Have you? Have you, really? Can you be sure?"

"I can function."

"He can too. Maybe not as well as you, not yet, but look how far you've both come already. I'll bet this time away will make things even better."

"It's so nice of you to do this."

"Come on, we're family."

"Awfully incestuous, aren't we?"

"Good to see you haven't lost your sense of humor."

"Some days it's all I have."

"It'll be OK, Brooke. I know it. You'll see. A little quiet time will do you both a world of good. It never hurts to get away for a bit."

"I can't tell you how much we appreciate this. You're a good friend."

"Not really."

"Don't say that."

"Marc's been a better friend to me over the years than

I've been to him. So have you. I'm not proud of that, it's just the way it is. Maybe I feel guilty. Maybe that's why I suggested this little getaway in the first place, so I could feel better about myself."

"That may be one reason, but we both know it's not the only one, so cut yourself some slack already."

"That's good advice. You should take it yourself."

"I'm doing my best."

"Marc is too, he just needs time. He's a tough guy, always has been—you know that as well as I do—but he's sensitive too. Too much sometimes, leaves him vulnerable. He's been like that since he was a kid."

"None of us can help who we are, I guess."

"Sometimes it's nice to pretend we can though, isn't it?"

"He's broken, Spaulding. He's damaged."

"Aren't we all?"

"Extent, that's the point."

"But you said the doctors told you there's nothing neurologically wrong."

"He had a severe concussion, but they've found no evidence of permanent neurological damage. The psychiatrist said the break Marc's suffering from is definitely emotional."

"What about you? Are you all right?"

"I'm getting there, but I'm more concerned with him. I want my husband back. I need him."

"He'll make it through this. No matter what, that's still him in there."

"But how much is left?"

The pills help to quell general anxiety and the majority of his obsessive thoughts, but this one lingers a while, fighting the chemical armies marching through his blood and transforming into the beginnings of anger before finally dissipating and leaving him. Though he's glad to see it go, Marc knows the anger will return in some other form, using some other means. It's only a matter of time. It won't stay gone. Not forever. Not without more pills. Not without more sleep. Not without more distance and time and alleged healing and everything else everyone assures him is just around the next bend in the road.

Brooke's found peace in some sense, or at least something approaching it. Why can't he? She's stronger than he is, always has been.

Maybe it's that simple.

Ironically, it is Spaulding who found Brooke. He dated her in high school first, albeit briefly, and it is Spaulding who first introduced her to Marc. For that alone Marc feels he owes him his life, friendship and undying loyalty. Even after all this time, as they close in on their fortieth birthdays, he can never repay that, and he knows it.

They both do.

Marc has always wondered how Brooke could've been attracted to both he and Spaulding, as even physically they're markedly different. Marc is shorter and more compact, with a subtly powerful build and Mediterranean features that reflect his Italian ancestry. On the rare occasions he's broached the subject over the years Brooke has always laughed it off. "The two relationships aren't even remotely comparable," she chuckles. "You and I fell in love quickly. I knew you were the one within days of meeting you. I've always loved Spaulding, but as boyfriend and girlfriend we were never good as you and me. As long as there is you, Spaulding and I make better friends than anything else."

"I've always thought Brooke was great," Spaulding has told him many times, "and I'd be lying if I said I wasn't attracted to her. She's smart and pretty and one of the sweetest people I've ever known. Of course I love her—always have and always will—but she's in love with you, Marc, not me. It's always been you."

In some ways this accounts for at least part of the tension that sometimes arises between the three. More often than not, they get along famously, as old friends should, but there are times when glimpses of the past reappear. They have always been a circle of three, with an understanding that no matter what, they'll be friends forever, but in the end the reality is that Marc and Brooke chose each other over him. While it's rarely discussed, Marc and Brooke both realize that in some ways, Spaulding has never completely recovered from it. He not only lost his girlfriend, he lost her to his best friend, and thus, lost them both. Had Marc and Brooke never fallen in love, surely their lives would've been different. If he'd remained Spaulding's faithful and unattached partner-in-crime, who knows what they may have accomplished together, what alternate paths their lives may have taken? Though Marc cannot imagine happiness without Brooke, he knows that for Spaulding, the scenario is an intriguing and often frustrating fantasy.

Now Marc wonders if Brooke thinks about it as well. She must.

Before the incident it never occurred to him that his wife might regret or question her life with him. Their marriage wasn't perfect, but they were happy. *She* was happy.

"How're we doing back there?" Spaulding asks, eyes watching from the rearview mirror.

Marc sees history in those eyes—years of friendship and joy, turmoil and pain, anger and resentment, fondness and regret—all of it swimming in deep hazel pools. "Why do you ask me that like I'm a child?"

Glancing back over her shoulder, Brooke gives her husband a gentle look of disapproval.

With a sigh, Marc returns his attention to the window

and colorful countryside beyond. "I'm good. Sorry."

"No worries." Spaulding smiles wide, his teeth long and straight but faded and vaguely stained from years of black coffee and cigarettes. He changes lanes and increases speed. "I apologize if I came off condescending, it wasn't intentional."

"So," Brooke says quickly, "tell us more about this place, it sounds great."

Marc settles deeper into the seat, folds his arms across his chest and does his best to maneuver away from the thoughts and indistinguishable sounds crowding his mind. He listens, albeit vaguely, as Spaulding discusses their eventual destination. Tucked away amidst hundreds of miles of rural countryside not far from the Catskill Mountains, the tiny hamlet of Dasgar, New York is roughly six and a half hours from their modest home on Cape Cod, and two hours upstate from New York City.

They still have several hours to go, but Marc tries not to think about that, as the longer he sits in the car the more restless he becomes.

"It's a contemporary chalet," Spaulding says with more enthusiasm in his tone than usual. "I've never been, but Scott—that's the owner, the guy I work with I was telling you about—showed me photos. Cathedral ceilings and glass doors, a wraparound deck, kitchen, full bath and two bedrooms down and a big loft up overlooking the first floor. It's set at the end of a gravel drive just off a country road that looks like something out of a Norman Rockwell painting—I kid you not—and it's on ten acres so it's very private. Absolutely beautiful area."

"How did you manage to secure it on such short notice?" Brooke asks.

"As if there's any limit to my uncanny powers of persuasion." Spaulding bounces his eyebrows at her playfully. "Plus, Scott owed me a favor for an account I straightened out for him a couple months ago. I knew he owned a spot in upstate New York and that he and the wife and kids only use it once or twice a year, so when he asked how he could repay me for bailing him out I asked if I could snag the place for a week. I thought it'd do us all some good."

Marc knows this conversation is largely for his benefit but he lets it go, allowing them to play their parts and say their lines without interruption. He's more concerned with the black clouds gathered on the horizon.

"It sounds wonderful." Brooke pivots and turns to the backseat, her expression animated and forced. "Doesn't it, honey?"

"Yeah," Marc answers softly, unable to look at her. "Great."

On cue, raindrops tap the windshield. He immediately hears what the others cannot—the true rhythm—the language of whispers within and behind them. Marc slides shut his eyes, tunes everything else out and listens more carefully. Unlike the whale songs he's yet to fully decode, this he understands. This he knows. But it saps him somehow, drains his energy until he feels like he's literally fading away and slipping into oblivion, transforming into a ghostly figure no longer visible to the naked eye. A defense mechanism, perhaps, a spiritual camouflage designed to protect him from that which hunts him even now.

Yet he remains. Flesh. Blood. Bone.

Vulnerable as ever, he conceals his soft white underbelly and hurries through the dark, narrow passageways of his mind.

This time it is not water that haunts him. It is fire. Horribly twisted visions of women in full black habits—nuns—in agony, chapped and bloody lips moving in silent prayer as men in frontier garb nail them to wooden crosses, strap them to trees and burn them alive. Fire burns through

Gardens of Night

the darkness. Hell has come to Earth on this bloody night. But this is no Salem. These are not lowly spinsters accused of witchcraft by vengeful children. These are alleged brides of Christ, messengers of the light, slaughtered like the Lamb of God they worship...

Across time, wind, rain, and the miles that separate Marc from a destiny he can never change, something summons him. It summons them all.

There, hidden in the rain. He can hear it so clearly now.

It's not human.

Two

Before, in the stillness of their lives, the quiet, there were times Marcus marveled at his happiness, wrapped himself in it like a blanket and snuggled beneath it to ward off the cold. He'd always expected a life more extravagant and exciting, but found himself content with the peaceful and relatively uneventful existence he and Brooke shared. Their lives had turned out positively ordinary—he the manager of a small office supply store, she an English teacher at the local high school—and far as he knew they could not have been happier.

He and Spaulding were friends first. They'd met in junior high school and struck up an unlikely bond. Tall even then, Spaulding was lanky, with narrow shoulders, a tiny waist and a mop of long curly brown 80s-rocker hair that gave him something of a feminine look, like some gangly runway model. But unlike those corpse-like models, with their vacant expressions and dead eyes, Spaulding possessed a dashing quality, an air of confidence, style and charm well beyond his years, which, when combined with his quick and often cutting wit and angular facial features—shamelessly curious eyes, a large crooked nose and a square jaw—resulted in a person everyone noticed and tended to have strong opinions about. As in his adult life since, in school few held neutral feelings when it came to Spaulding Smith. He was either adored or reviled, and usually with good reason. Though not wildly popular in school, Spaulding did have a small circle of friends and was without question their self-appointed leader. His interests primarily involved books, movies, music and the drama club. Despite how awful most school productions turned out to be, Spaulding worked tirelessly and with great enthusiasm on each one, toiling behind-the-scenes with lighting, sound or operating the curtain, and sometimes even appearing as an actor. Although he often presented himself like a sophisticated man-of-the-world, in reality he came from modest means. Like Marc's family, his was working-class and not exactly the yacht club type, but unlike Marc, Spaulding always seemed ashamed of it and for some reason had the need to be more complicated and urbane than most.

While Spaulding honed his larger-than-life persona, Marc remained a socially withdrawn, subversive kid who seemed to revel in his role as the school's antiestablishment rebel. In high school he'd briefly been a member of both the football and baseball teams but was never the typical jock type. In fact, he had few friends and rarely associated with his teammates socially. Unlike Spaulding, who thrived in the high school environment, Marc found school boring, unfulfilling and often maddening in its hypocrisy. Though bright, he preferred to self-educate, and even as a young man, looked ahead to a time where rather than slogging from class to class he could go out into the world and make a life for himself. In the dream, he'd eventually settle down and have a usual life, marry a brilliant, beautiful and adoring woman who truly understood him, they'd have some kids—two maybe, a boy and a girl—get a dog and a cat, a nice place to live, a couple cars and a happy, quiet life. But until then he'd defy convention and boldly experience everything he'd set out to do on his own terms, to the beat of his own drummer, and find his place in a world he'd always felt out of synch with. He had no idea what that might entail, and perhaps that's what was so appealing about it. He'd always loved to write, and often penned short stories he never let anyone read but Spaulding. Maybe, he often mused, he'd be another Jack Kerouac.

At times Marc's desires complimented Spaulding's, who also planned to do everything, go everywhere and live an exciting and adventure-filled life. But unlike Marc, Spaulding not only wanted to be part of the establishment, he planned to rule and exploit it for his own purposes. He was going to be a movie star or perhaps a famous playwright, and of course expected his best friend to share in these plans and to accompany him. When Marc resisted lusting after many of the same things, Spaulding could never understand why, and often scolded him for it.

"My God," he'd say, "get some focus, will you? You remind me of Brando in *The Wild One* when he's asked what he's rebelling against and he answers, 'what've you got?' There's no point if you're subversive just to be subversive. Why would you want to be Kerouac when you could be M. R. Banyon! " Spaulding had already decided that if Marc were to become a writer he should use *M. R.* rather than Marcus and Robert, his first and middle names. "There's a whole world out there, Marc. Things to see and experience, places to go, people to meet, a life to live, and if you don't get your shit together you'll end up in this nowhere town doing some nowhere job, got it? So fuck that. We're getting out of here. We're going to do great things, you watch."

Spaulding never suspected that what was really in store for him was a two-year stint at a local community college, and after earning an Associate's in Accounting, a series of unrewarding jobs and eventually a humdrum career at a huge corporation in Boston, and then, after being transferred a few years later, Chicago. He'd had a few serious relationships but none lasting, and the older he got the more likely it seemed Spaulding would spend his life as a bachelor.

Sadly, as they all creep into their early forties, it no longer seems likely but certain, because while he can be caring and loving, at times Spaulding can also be remarkably difficult to get along with. He's never outgrown the desire (perhaps the need) to constantly be the center of attention; voices his vast opinions in no uncertain terms and usually with a condescending edge, and possesses bitterness toward life which generally manifests in drinking binges. Combined with the perpetual egocentric habits of a long-single person, and his constant need to feel superior to everyone he comes into contact with, the result has caused numerous difficulties over the years not only with those he dates but the friendships he tries yet consistently fails to maintain.

All these years later, he and Marc talk on the phone quite a bit but only see each other two or three times a year when Spaulding flies in for holidays, vacations or other special occasions.

Still, Marc and Brooke remain his best friends… arguably, his only friends.

For Brooke and Marc, their life together has developed and strengthened gradually over the years, evolving from high school sweethearts to a mature married couple. While Marc went to work at the office supply store, Brooke attended college locally, chasing her dreams of one day becoming a teacher. Just prior to Brooke's graduation, Marc was finally named store manager, and after a lengthy engagement, they were married a year later and set off on a life together. Things seemed to get better with each passing year. Brooke furthered her education, then landed a job teaching at a high school a town away, and by the time she and Marc were thirty they'd bought a modest but nice two-bedroom colonial in a quiet neighborhood at the end of a cul-de-sac in town. His cigarette-smoking, black-leather-jacket-wearing, too-cool-for-school guise a pleasant memory, Marc took some college creative writing courses and had a few short stories published by the time he'd hit thirty, but his writing had never amounted to much. Still somewhat antiestablishment, age had softened him a bit, and he'd come to grips with the idea that he'd never be Kerouac or anything even close. Spaulding had been right. He'd wound up himself, locked in a life equal parts contentment and silent disillusionment. Three completed novels filled a desk drawer at home, but they'd all been rejected numerous times by nearly every publisher on the planet. Though deeply disappointed, in time he learned to live with his failure as a writer and rebel extraordinaire and did his best to fully focus on his job and marriage instead.

He and Brooke lived humbly and happily.

The only real sore spot in their lives was the matter of children. Both wanted kids, but not long after they'd been married and trying for several months, a visit to the doctor revealed that Marc was sterile. They were both devastated, but Brooke reminded him that they could always adopt, skillfully masking her pain as she so often did. They had each other and were deeply in love, that's what was important, she'd said, and while he believed that to the very core of his being, for the first time in his life he felt like he'd failed not only himself, but his wife.

He hadn't known then that it was only the beginning.

They discussed adoption on and off over the next few years but decided to wait. Two decades later they were still waiting, still talking about it now and then as if it might be a real possibility, and perhaps before the incident, it had been.

The envy of their friends and families, they are the only couple who has managed to stay together over the years, as sadly all their other friends who married around the same time are long-divorced or separated. A little more than a year ago they celebrated their nineteenth wedding anniversary, and anything seemed possible. Happiness was more than a luxury, it was a certainty. But neither could've suspected their twentieth would take place amidst such sorrow.

Celebrated a few months prior, it was a quiet and forced affair. A few close friends and family gathered; there was a cake, some champagne and uncomfortable small talk. Though Brooke was hardly herself either, and he will never forget how drawn and pale she'd been that day, Marc was without question the eight-hundred-pound gorilla in the room and everyone knew it. Just back from the hospital, as it turned out he'd only last at home a few more days before having to return. Spaulding had called and apologized for not being able to make it. He'd previously booked an elaborate vacation to Europe and wouldn't be back in time.

Brooke was annoyed with him for missing it, as she thought his presence might help aid in Marc's recovery, but Marc felt it was just as well. He didn't want Spaulding to see him like that.

The present version, Marc thinks, is pathetic enough.

His second return home from the hospital was better than the first, and it looked like he might make it. Marc decided to fake his way through things if need be, but he's never going back there again. He has to find a way to live outside those horrible walls or die trying. He decided this on his last night there, lying in that awful hard bed with the crisp sheets that smell like bleach, staring at cracks in the ceiling and listening to his roommate in the next bed snore and gurgle like a broken faucet.

Like every night, they'd given him medication to help

him sleep. While it left him groggy, he's certain even now that he was still awake when the door to the room opened and the dark figure entered. Light from the hallway split the shadows to reveal a petite nurse in full uniform and cap. He remembers thinking it odd to see a nurse wearing a cap, as none on the ward he'd seen previously had done so. He also remembers thinking she must be a new edition to the nightshift because he'd never seen her before.

As the door slowly closed behind her, moonlight seeping through the lone window in the room washed across her face. Perhaps thirty, she was one of the most breathtakingly beautiful women he had ever seen. Her hair was raven black and pinned up beneath the cap, her complexion flawless and her eyes large, soulful and such a deep brown that they too bordered on black.

The allure of her body was evident even beneath the featureless polyester uniform.

Marc lay still, head flat against the pillow, unable to take his eyes from her. The ward was unusually quiet that night. No moans, no screams, no footfalls of attendants or nurses hurrying back and forth along the corridors or the occasional murmur of conversation from the nearby nurse's station just down the hall. It was so quiet, in fact, he wondered if he might be dreaming after all. But then the nurse moved across the room with a fluid stride, stopping next to his bed, her stunning eyes gazing down at him with equal parts loveliness and intensity.

Despite her beauty, there was something strange about this woman.

Something disturbing.

Marc noticed a tattoo of a serpent coiled around her left wrist, the tail extending across her palm and the head reaching to the beginnings of her forearm. The snake's body was gray and thick, its tongue protruding and forked. She saw him looking at it and nodded, like this should mean something to him, a secret now shared. A tantalizing though subtle odor emanated from the woman, something similar to perfume but unlike anything he'd smelled before. It left him dizzy and intoxicated with lust, and Marc felt himself stir beneath the bed sheets and grow hard despite his best efforts to prevent it. The woman noticed this as well, glancing with amusement at the tented sheets. She smiled, parting her full lips to reveal gorgeous, perfect, brilliantly white teeth.

"The pills they give you," she said in a soft voice, "they make you dream, don't they?"

"Yes."

"They're not dreams." As she leaned closer, bending forward, her hand reached for him, clutched the head of his erection and squeezed through the sheets. "Do you understand?"

He moaned uncontrollably as an orgasm exploded from him, wracking his body with shivers and a flood of ecstasy the likes of which he'd never known or even imagined possible. It was so intense he literally blacked out at one point, only to come awake and find her still there, still watching him, her hands back at her sides.

Even as he tried to catch his breath and stop his body from trembling, a wave of guilt surged through him. He hadn't had sexual contact with anyone but Brooke in years. He hadn't wanted this but had been unable to help it, unable to resist it. The mere touch of this woman had sent him over the edge. How was that even possible?

"Who are you?" he gasped. "Why did you do that?"

"Listen to the things you'll soon hear," the nurse told him in the same soft voice, her eyes boring into him. "Pay attention to the things you'll soon see."

Marc felt himself nod but was still unable to move or raise his head from the pillow. "You're not a nurse," he said as she moved away. "You're not…"

She stopped at the door, and again draped in shadow, looked back at him. Slowly, she raised a finger to her lips. "Shhh."

Once she'd slipped back into the hallway and the door had closed behind her, Marc was able to sit up. Though still lightheaded from the orgasm and woozy from the meds, he managed to roll from bed and stagger to the door.

The hallway was empty, the woman gone.

The snores of his roommate brought him back. He closed the door and padded quietly to his bed. His pajama bottoms were wet and stained, and he could feel semen trickling along the insides of his upper thighs. Ashamed, he went in search of a towel with which to clean himself, but something in the corner of his peripheral vision caught the moonlight. It glistened for just a moment, long enough to draw his eyes to it. There, in the window, an intricate silk web with a small spider suspended from it. Though Marc had always disliked and feared spiders, he stood mesmerized, unable to look away or think of anything else.

Listen to the things you'll soon hear.

And he understood in that split-second that something was taking place he could neither explain nor deny. He didn't know how or even why, but there in the moonlight, staring up at a spider and its elaborate web, Marc knew something somewhere was attempting to communicate with him through this tiny creature.

They're not dreams.

The spider suddenly scurried up along its snare, changing position as if for a better look at the moon dangling just beyond the window. Or perhaps a better look at him.

Marc felt the hair on the back of his neck stand on end.

Do you understand?

"God help me," he whispered. "Yes."

Gardens of Night

    From that night forward Marc realizes that no matter how many pills they give him or tests they administer or therapy sessions they make him sit through, he cannot be sane in that place. He can only be sane if he's free, and he can only be free if he's with Brooke. He needs to wake up next to her and look at her face, because when he looks at her he sees everything he needs to know. It's all right there, secrets, lies and truth.
    Marc especially likes to look at her while she sleeps. Or in those quietly breathless moments right after they've made love, when her eyes are closed, her chest rises and falls in steady, exaggerated rhythm, and she gently moistens her lips with her tongue, running it over them with unintentional eroticism again and again. He loves the way her breasts are still slick with perspiration, nipples taut, stomach sunken, arms draped across her forehead, legs held slightly apart and toes pointed. But most of all, he loves the way her eyes move rapidly beneath the lids as if she's in the throes of REM sleep, her mind conscious and aware but still dreaming of not-so-distant moments when they'd held each other tight, he'd been inside her and her breath had escaped in whispers and quick tiny gasps.
    Now those eyes search for the love, the happiness, the safety they'd known before, and he can only wonder what Brooke really sees and feels when she opens those eyes and looks at *his* face. Does she still hear the screams too?
    Does she hear him crying, weeping like a child?
    Curtains of blood and tears part, return him to the backseat of Spaulding's rental car. Windshield wipers wag back and forth, the sky darkens and the rain falls harder. The sedan, a capsule of metal and plastic and glass, rockets along the highway and through the storm. Gone is Spaulding's mane, his hair cut short and styled professionally like any good corporate employee. The unique look of his youth

replaced with something mundane, infinitely less interesting, and unfortunately, wholly necessary. It's true for all of them, of course, but seems more pronounced in him. The lines in his face have deepened more than theirs, and his temples are sprinkled with negligible flecks of gray that could pass for rumors. Both serve to give Spaulding a mature and stable appearance, though arguably he's neither.

Armor, Marc thinks; memories of the night nurse drifting through his mind.

"It won't save you," she whispers from deep inside him.

It won't save any of them.

Three

He first sees him in the rearview mirror, a blurred silhouette standing in the driveway. Marc cannot make out any features, as the sun setting in the distance behind the man obscures all but his outline. He's big, at least six-three or four with what appears to be a rugged build, yet Marc didn't see him when he pulled the car into the driveway. The man has apparently walked in behind them, but how did he not see him beforehand?

Brooke notices him staring at the mirror. "What's wrong?"

"There's a man in the driveway."

She turns and looks over her shoulder. "What's he doing?"

"Just standing there."

Marc squints, hoping for a better look. They're familiar with everyone in their small neighborhood, and even with a limited view he's certain this is a stranger. Night is falling fast, rolling in and following behind the man like a black wave.

"Who is it?"

"Not sure." Marc sighs. "Probably a salesman or someone lost and looking for directions or something."

He tells Brooke to stay put, and the moment he steps

from the car, Marc feels something in the air, a palpable tension the likes of which he's never before experienced. He's not afraid. But he should be.

ಬಂಡ

He awakens to the whirl of blue lights and realizes he's been asleep for some time. *I didn't dream*, he thinks. The whales have abandoned him. Or, as he continues deeper into upstate New York, is he simply too far away, the ocean too great a distance for them to reach him? It's dark out, and though the rain has stopped, the roads are slick and recent raindrops still dot the car windows. The lights are captivating—beautiful and threatening all at once—but oddly distorted. Marc wipes at his eyes, mistaking this for another instance when he'd gazed at similar lights through a haze of blood and misery. This time his blurred vision is simply a remnant of sleep and quickly dissipates.

"What's all this then?" he hears Spaulding say as the car creeps to a stop.

At some earlier point they left the highway for a more rural road, and have now come upon a roadblock. Numerous state police vehicles line either side of the road and several officers wield flashlights while milling about in rain gear. An ambulance and fire engine are parked to one side, their red lights blending with those from the police cars and casting the entire scene in an otherworldly pale. The colored beams sweep through the thick forest on either side of the road in continuous patterns, as if some alien spacecraft has landed in the nearby woods.

Marc cocks his head and gazes up at the night sky. Enormous trees loom overhead, the tops cutting shadows across a hazy moon already masked in clouds. He imagines it stained and dripping with blood.

"Oh my God," Brooke says.

A car has overturned in a ditch along the side of the road. Glass and debris is scattered across a wide area, and there are two bodies nearby. One is covered with a sheet. The second is surrounded by EMTs.

The police, using flashlights to point the way for drivers, direct their car and the two in front of them through the narrow space available, and soon the accident scene is behind them, the lights fading in the darkness and distance.

"That's certainly sobering," Spaulding mutters.

Brooke offers a weary nod. "I hope that other person makes it."

"Let's hope so," he agrees, though he sounds less than optimistic.

"I only saw the one car, they must've lost control."

"Probably going too fast." He glances at the GPS unit on the dash. "Between the rain and the bends in these back roads it's treacherous going."

"At least the rain's let up."

"Yes, but the roads are still slick."

Brooke pinches the bridge of her nose and squeezes shut her eyes.

"Are you *praying*?" Spaulding asks.

"I'm saying a Hail Mary for whoever that person is."

"Oh, how Catholic." His is a light but dismissive laugh.

"You were raised Catholic too."

"Yes, and I'm still recovering."

"No harm in sending good thoughts, is there?"

"No, but I thought you stopped attending services years ago."

"I did, except for Christmas. We still go to midnight mass sometimes."

"Well, isn't that quaint?"

"Don't be so patronizing." She playfully slaps Spaulding's shoulder. "Some of us still believe, you know."

"In what, silly fairy tales, bedtime stories for the feebleminded?"

"Oh, OK, I'm feebleminded now?"

"Let's face it, Brookie, you've always been a little slow."

"Funny, last time I checked *I* was the one with the master's degree."

"Ouch."

"Don't mess with me, office boy."

As they continue joking back and forth, Marc remains quiet, hidden in the darkness of the backseat. He's never before realized the extent to which he loves the sound of Brooke's laughter. It's a wonderful sound he's missed terribly, and though she and Spaulding are engaged in little more than deflecting fears of their own mortality, he'll take it even under such spurious circumstances.

Marc turns and looks out the back window. The swirling lights are gone, swallowed by night.

For some reason he thinks of the store just then, specifically, the tiny lights on the alarm he'd set each night at closing. It's been months since he's been to work or even set foot in the store. Brooke took a leave of absence from her job as well, and they've been living the past few months by tapping into her teacher's retirement and the small disability payments Marc receives, but unlike him she plans to return to work after the first of the year, in just a few months. She'd have returned sooner had she been able—her job has always been something of a sanctuary for her—but she knows someone has to watch over her husband. Like some helpless and irresponsible child who can't be left alone, Marc thinks.

In a perfect world he'd return to his job too, and

everything would go back to the way it was before. But the longer he stays away, the less likely that all seems. Garth Petrie, the owner, gave Marc's assistant the position of manager once it was clear Marc would be unable to report to work for an extended period. "It's only temporary," Garth said when he'd stopped by the house to give Marc the news. "You know, until you're back." Garth has always been fair with Marc, treats him right and takes care of him, and while Marc certainly doesn't owe Garth anything—he's slaved at the store for years and has always been a reliable and dedicated employee—he knows he's not only let Garth and his staff down, but himself as well by having to go on disability. Willis, Marc's assistant manager at the store, has worked there a little over two years. He knows Willis will do fine but still feels guilty not being able to do the job himself. After all, Marc spent years working his way up into the manager's position. Now it seems such a waste, so totally pointless. Maybe it is. Maybe it always has been.

It's only temporary.

No, he thinks. Nothing's temporary. *Everything* lasts forever, especially things that ought not to.

Time passes. Marc cannot be sure how much, but some time later Spaulding announces, "We're here!"

The sound of his voice snaps Marc's concentration, and he focuses on the rumble of the car as it rolls along the suddenly uneven terrain of a long and narrow driveway. Covered in white gravel, the stones pierce the darkness like shards of glowing bone strewn about the earth.

As Marc wonders how many skeletons it might take to produce the amount of bone necessary to cover that much ground, the car comes to a stop.

Even bathed in obscure moonlight and the harsh gaze of car headlights, the small chalet looks like something out of a fairytale. Set on a secluded and well-maintained piece of densely-wooded property, beyond which lie a series of distant hills, it waits amidst the forest as if just for them.

The rain kicks in again, pummeling the car and falling even harder than before. Spaulding kills the engine but leaves the headlights on.

"It's beautiful," Brooke says, looking back at Marc as if for validation.

"Yeah," he answers, doing his best to sound animated, "very nice."

Spaulding rummages through his pockets until he finds the key to the front door then pops the trunk with a release mechanism next to the steering wheel and shuts off the lights. "No way to do this without getting drenched, kids, so let's just grab the bags and make a mad dash for the door."

"Careful not to melt now," Brooke teases, "being made of sugar and all."

"Bite me."

"I'll need a far more substantial meal, I'm starving."

"Let's get inside and see what we can rustle up."

"Rustle up? Oh, how *quaint*."

"Did I mention you could bite me?"

Beginning with her middle finger, Brooke playfully counts to three and they all jump from the car, run to the trunk, retrieve their suitcases and bolt for the chalet. She laughs effortlessly, the sound of her joy filtered through rain as her sneakers splash puddles. Spaulding laughs too, saying something Marc can't quite make out as he runs along behind him for the deck steps.

As Spaulding and Brooke hurry up the steps and huddle near the door, Marc comes to an abrupt stop just shy of the chalet. His eyes pan from the dark sky to the surrounding forest to the outlying hills. Rain crashes down, but he makes no move to escape it. There's something beautiful here, clean and powerful. He smiles, feels rainwater pour over his eyes, across his face and into his mouth.

"Marc?" Brooke calls from the now open doorway, a flood of light appearing behind her inside the chalet, "come on, you're getting soaked!"

He stays where he is, his suitcase dangling by his side. An abundance of aromas waft about. He breathes them in. The trees, the grass, the soil beneath, the dying leaves and the night air—all of it moist and wet and dripping—he can smell them all in a single intense rush that throttles his senses and leaves him lightheaded and breathless. But he is not frightened. Rather, he feels thoroughly alive and connected; a part of something so much larger and profound than he that his mind cannot quite fully grasp it. The sensation reminds him of his dreams, of the whales and their beautiful melancholy songs, a surface he has only begun to scratch, one hiding countless secrets that lie beneath.

෩෬

Brooke and Marc take the loft bedroom and Spaulding throws his things in the larger of the two downstairs bedrooms. The chalet is every bit as beautiful as Spaulding described, and is clean, neat and fully furnished with modest but practical furniture and accouterments, including a small brick hearth and fireplace on the back wall. There is electricity, indoor plumbing and a woodstove for heat, but no telephone or television, only a countertop radio in the kitchen and a small stereo in the main room. The cupboards are bare but for seasonings and the like, and the refrigerator houses a box of baking soda, two plastic jugs of water and a few condiments.

Thankfully, Spaulding has packed and brought along

a double-pack of Mrs. Grass's Chicken Soup mix, a loaf of Italian bread and a bottle of White Zinfandel. "This is to hold us over for tonight."

"Nice. Good night for soup." Brooke selects a pan from those hanging above an island in the kitchen area, fills it with water then fires up the gas stove.

"See?" Spaulding points to his temple. "Always thinking."

"I was wondering what that smell was."

"Side-splitting. In the morning we'll drive into town and get some groceries. According to Scott, downtown Dasgar is only about fifteen minutes from here. I'm sure it's quite the bustling metropolis."

"They must have a general store or grocer or *something.*"

"I'm sure." He yanks his Blackberry free of his belt. "OK, there's no landline so let's do a quick phone check."

Brooke tests her cell phone as well. They both get moderate though useable signals. Marc, lethargically standing by a pair of sliding glass doors that lead to the back deck, leaves his hands in his pockets. He hasn't had the use of his cell in months. The nurse checking him in took it from him when he'd first entered the hospital and he hasn't seen it since. Far as he knows they returned it to Brooke along with his other personal belongings and she tucked it away in a drawer somewhere at home. He isn't even sure it still has service. What difference does it make? Who would he call? Who would call him? He's damaged, after all, and nothing drives people away quite so fast.

For some reason he imagines it ringing anyway, the sound muffled and drifting unanswered through lifeless and empty rooms back in Massachusetts. There is something at once sad and funny about this, as they all stand around beneath artificial light in what seems to Marc like some giant pretend cabin so far from home, tucked away in pristine woodland conjured in the mind of a whimsical child.

Outside, the rain keeps coming, angrily crashing the chalet and spraying the sliders with forest debris and dead leaves. They all pretend not to notice how violent it's become, how stifled and imprisoned it makes them feel. Brooke flits about in search of bowls and silverware, and upon locating both, sets the table. Spaulding appears from the bedroom a moment later with a squat candle, places it in the center of the table, and lights it with a match from a box he finds next to the fireplace. Marc stays out of the way, wandering aimlessly about the main room, taking it all in and doing his best to work through the static clogging his mind. He wants desperately to hone in on something—anything—other than this cerebral white noise, but the storm is blocking either him or those trying to communicate, he can't be sure which.

"Headache?"

Marc looks to the kitchen, meets his wife's concerned gaze. "Just a little one, I'm OK."

"I've got Tylenol in my purse if you need it."

"I think once I eat I'll be fine," he answers, strolling toward the fireplace, his attention now locked on an unusual but attractive rug tacked onto the wall above it. Native American, he assumes by the patterns and design, but it is the intricacy that fascinates him.

Spaulding suddenly appears by his side, the bottle of White Zinfandel held high like a trophy, "All right, who wants wine?"

"Not allowed," Marc tells him. "Can't have booze with the meds I'm on."

"I'm sorry," he says, moving away. "Jesus, I should've known that, I—"

"Don't sweat it, you guys have some."

Spaulding looks to Brooke as if for her permission.

She gives a subtle nod and pours the soup mix into the now boiling water.

An awkward tension hangs in the air as Spaulding searches the cupboards for glasses. He begins babbling about some woman he works with, and how she drinks on the job and hides bottles of gin in her desk drawer and how it's so sad but no one knows what to do or how to approach her about it.

It seems an odd story to tell just then, but perhaps that's all he's got handy.

Brooke sips some broth and raves about how good it is. She's trying so hard, Marc thinks. Too hard really, but she needs to find her way through this too, and all the while with him tied around her neck like dead weight.

She looks so beautiful there in the kitchen, in her jeans and sneakers, her figure thin and lithe, small breasts strained against a tight blouse, short dirty blonde hair mussed, windblown and still damp from the rain, brown eyes wide and hopeful, as if no harm could ever come to her. As if none ever has.

Though Marc can see through her carefully constructed facade, he envies her nonetheless. At least she's capable of creating one. Still, he'd give anything to see Brooke like she was before, like they both were.

But that's no longer possible.

The sudden and uneasy feeling of being watched causes Marc to train his eyes on the glass sliders along the back wall.

Somewhere out there, in the dark and rain, he senses something. Beyond the trees, on the far side of the hills, something waits…

Something evil.

Marc feels it so strongly his fingers begin to tingle as if asleep. The sensation spreads into his forearms, shoulders and neck. So as not to draw attention to himself, he leaves his hands at his sides but clenches them into fists. The pins and needles gradually recede.

Visions of fire flicker through his mind. Fire from torches and burning crosses, held aloft by a group of women shrouded in black habits standing in a line at the summit of a large hill. As if in formation, they are silent and still as statues, their flames impossibly bright in an otherwise impenetrably dark night.

Pay attention to the things you'll soon see.

They shouldn't have come here. But they never really had a choice.

He knows this now. In a way, he always has.

Four

The three sit at the table eating soup while fates unseen swirl about in curious patterns like microscopic organisms floating in air. Now and then Spaulding or Brooke says something, but it's forced and awkward and silence creeps back in, a slow wave slinking to shore. Marc stays quiet, listens to the rain instead and glances at shadows cast along the floor. *Their* shadows, like painted sentries. Through the rain-sounds Spaulding decides to take another shot at conversation and tosses out a sure winner: politics. But they're all progressives, so he's more or less preaching to the choir. Still, it's effective, Marc thinks, because it occupies them and allows him an escape from rainstorms and chalets and the memories of whales that have stopped speaking to him.

Yet what he escapes to is no better. Perhaps it's worse.

His psychiatrist's office comes to him just then, as if to prove the point, and though he knows why, he pretends not to. A bit cramped but decorated to radiate a false sense of warmth, the office reminds Marc of a theater set. Not quite real, but close. Much like Doctor Berry, who at least for him, only exists within those four walls. For some reason he cannot picture her anywhere else, and often imagines her sitting in her high-back chair waiting quietly in the dark, hoping to come alive again soon as he or some other lost soul crosses the threshold of her alleged sanctuary. He does not envy her predicament. She may not be a patient in that lockdown facility they call a hospital, but she's trapped there too. While she goes home at night and lives out whatever life beyond that awful place she has, in the end she always returns, as much a prisoner of the institution as anyone, shackled to the mysteries and tears of an old building that's been dead since before her birth.

"*Sometimes I pretend they were angels.*"

"*Do you believe in angels, Marc?*"

"*Not the kind that float around on clouds blowing kisses and handing out advice to lonely housewives and elderly shut-ins.*"

"*What kind of angels do you believe in then?*"

"*The ones described in most ancient texts are warriors. They're brutal, merciless and carry out God's wishes without question. They flatten cities and slaughter thousands, all in His name. Part of me respects them. Their love for God is unconditional, and they believe the violence He orders is necessary. They see beauty in the horror they wreak, purity.*"

"*Do you believe God is vengeful, that He punishes us?*"

"*I believe He pulls us from the wreckage. Only we kick and fight like a bird that's been injured and doesn't understand you're trying to help it. It only knows it wants to get away from you because it fears you. It doesn't understand you're there to save it.*"

"*Marc, are you telling me that you believe God sent angels to save you and Brooke through the use of violence?*"

"*No. But I wish He had.*"

Rain interrupts his reverie, returns him to the table and the soup and Spaulding's endless antiwar diatribe. Eyes wide, Brooke listens intently, as if he's the most fascinating person on Earth. Sipping wine between occasional swallows of broth, she nods her head whenever he makes a compelling point.

"Why are you here?" Marc asks suddenly. He hadn't meant to say this aloud but it's too late to take it back. He puts his spoon in his bowl, lets it go and watches as it disappears into the murky broth.

Surprised that his speech has been interrupted, Spaulding arches an eyebrow and leans back in his chair a bit. "I'm sorry?"

In a halfhearted attempt at escape, Brooke grabs her bowl and heads for the counter. "Anybody want seconds?"

"Why are you here?" Marc asks again.

"I don't understand," Spaulding says through an inconsequential chuckle. "You mean why did I come with you guys?"

"It's a simple question. Why are you here?"

"Marc," Brooke says, managing to find a shred of patience amidst her embarrassment, "you're being rude, there's no need to—"

"No, it's OK." Spaulding holds a hand up to silence her. "You two were more than welcome to use the place on your own. I just thought it'd be nice if we all got together. Why, would you rather be alone with Brooke?"

"I'd rather you answer my question."

Spaulding draws a deep breath. "I thought spending some time together would be beneficial, seeing how we haven't done anything like this in ages."

Brooke turns her back to them, puts her bowl in the sink and rinses it out.

Marc pushes away from the table and stands, his eyes on the sliders. Despite the ferocity of the rain, dead leaves stick to the glass. He knows exactly how they feel.

"Marc," Spaulding says, "I'm here because I thought it might help you."

"No, you're not."

Baffled, he looks briefly to Brooke for support then turns back to Marc. "You don't think I'm here to *hurt* you, do you?"

"No," he answers softly. "I don't think you're here at all."

※

The loft features a large skylight on the sloped ceiling, a faux bearskin rug and an oak bedroom set. Marc sits at the foot of the bed and takes it all in. Like the rest of the chalet, it is disturbingly immaculate. He envisions a horde of uniformed maids converging on the property day after day, cleaning maniacally; tending to a woodland version of Dunsinane. But there is no trace of anyone here. In fact everything appears unused and has an impersonal, nearly sterile feel, and Marc senses nothing in this room, hears nothing but the storm. As he gazes up at the rain-blurred portal he can't be certain if this is good or bad.

Until the rain and impenetrable night beyond becomes something else.

The vision of someone on the roof stretched out over the skylight and gawking down at him with feral eyes flashes through his mind, but there is no one there. Still, as one might hear barely audible whispers, he senses something sinister. Something… *out there*… not close, but not too far either.

And it knows… somehow it knows he's there too.

Brooke appears at the head of the stairs. With a frown

she joins him on the bed. She sits close but doesn't touch him. Marc looks at the floor and prepares to be reprimanded. "You really hurt Spaulding's feelings," she says in a quiet voice. "And now he thinks he's intruding and that you don't want him here."

"He'll be fine."

"That's not the point. He arranged all of this for us, for you."

"I'll apologize in the morning," he says, vaguely repentant.

"Why did you say that to him, Marc?"

He shrugs.

"Do you want one of your pills? You won't feel so agitated."

"I'm not agitated." He places his hands in hers. She doesn't resist but he can feel the tension in her. "I'm just going to go to bed."

"Need something to help you sleep?"

Why is she always so eager to anesthetize him? "No, thanks," he says, releasing her.

She nods, chooses to believe what she knows is a lie. "OK, get some rest then. I'll be up in a bit."

Before Brooke returns to the downstairs she removes sweatpants and a sweatshirt from Marc's suitcase, and meaning well, lays them across the foot of the bed for him. They kiss goodnight as they often do of late, with a brief and soulless peck on the lips. Though genuine love remains, the gesture lacks the luster it once possessed, the passion, the power. Like the moon in daylight, he thinks, despite its profound beauty it seems clumsy and out of place.

Holding tight to blurry yesterdays he knows will only temporarily mend him, Marc undresses once she's gone, changes into the nightclothes, steps into a pair of moccasin slippers then pulls back the bed sheets. He switches off the nightstand lamp, returning the loft to darkness, but rather than go to bed he moves to the banister. When he reaches the open staircase he crouches down, careful to remain hidden in shadow, and presses his face between two balusters so he can look down into the main room of the chalet.

This reminds Marc of his childhood, and more specifically, his mother. When he was a child and it was time for bed his mother would watch him ascend the stairs to his bedroom and stick her face through the balusters, giving him a kiss with each step until she could no longer reach. Marc can remember gazing down lovingly at his mother, who had switched to blowing kisses by then, smiling and saying, "Goodnight, honey. Mommy loves you."

His parents are retired and live in Florida. Marc seldom sees them. He misses his father but misses his mother's kisses even more. He misses those phrases; that love and the simple, quiet evenings of his childhood.

Blurring, his mother's face drifts away, morphs into the room below.

Brooke sits on the couch and Spaulding joins her a moment later, carrying a lit candle and two glasses. He places them on the coffee table next to the bottle of wine they began at dinner and are now apparently determined to finish. Marc can hear their voices but only catches every third or fourth word, as they're speaking softly, presumably so as not to disturb him. Coupled with the rain, he has no hope of deciphering their conversation, so he watches their expressions and body language instead. In that moment, as Brooke kicks off her shoes and stretches her legs, his wife reminds him of friends of theirs who have kids, the way they relax and slump with relief into comfortable, more natural positions once the children have been put to bed.

Spaulding pours them each another glass of wine. They click their glasses together and drink. He does most of the talking, gesturing with his hands as he tends to do. He offers frequent, wry smiles, rolls his eyes and kicks back, turning his body into the corner of the couch so he can face Brooke comfortably. He says something about making a fire, or perhaps getting the woodstove going, as it and the fireplace are the only sources of heat the chalet has. She responds, best as Marc can tell, that it's not necessary, the candle and wine will do fine for tonight. The only other light downstairs now is one in the kitchen, which bleeds slightly into the main room, casting a narrow swathe near the sliders. Otherwise Brooke and Spaulding are bathed in shadow and the flicker of the candle's flame. Marc can't remember the last time he's seen her so relaxed. She almost looks at peace.

Almost.

Or is it safety she feels just then? The possibility alone breaks his heart.

As he watches them, Marc notices their interactions, how as old friends they're so at ease with each other that their moves are distinctly familiar and can be read, deciphered and countered by rote. And yet this *thing* lurks in the corner, hovers in the air—the incident—a plague visited upon their lives that has forever changed things. Evil and divine both, it has at once wrought destruction and regeneration; melding it all into a single fiery, twisted effigy, a smoking and bloody sacrifice set before indifferent gods. Though he knows it's puerile to hide in the dark, snooping on them like an overprotective, preposterously covetous husband, Marc remains where he is.

As rain lashes the chalet he feels himself fading away even more, slowly dying, transforming into a dream, a wisp of smoke, a garden of night, concealed and unseen, roots like chains burrowing deep into dark soil and shackling him to horrors that should've destroyed him by now. He is a ghost, tethered to the Earth and unable to break free.

Twisting and turning in space, an astronaut dead in his suit, he drifts aimlessly into different and happier times when he would've been down there with them, drinking a cocktail and talking the night away. When he thinks of the times the three of them have spent together over the years, as opposed to the times they spent as pairs, there are of course similarities, but also marked differences. His remembrances of them as a threesome yield many things. There were bad or melancholy times for sure, but mostly the memories are happy ones. He recalls silly, carefree exploits, amazing conversation, intellectual (and at times sexual) tension, and an intense camaraderie he has never felt with anyone else. But mostly he remembers laughter. As Brooke grins at something Spaulding tells her, Marc is reminded of their teenage years. Though very bright even then, she was still somewhat shy, soft-spoken and lacking in confidence. But being around Marc and Spaulding awakened a free spirit in her that had been previously suppressed due to her strict upbringing and relatively humorless home life, and she'd never looked back. Marc remembers one episode in particular when they'd gotten stoned out of their minds on some high-end Hawaiian weed Spaulding scored, piled into Brooke's beat-up Toyota Corolla then hit the local grocery store on a quest for munchies. Two steps into the parking lot Spaulding decided breaking into a song-and-dance number straight out of *Cabaret* was a really good idea. Before he could finish, Brooke, who shared Spaulding's love of musicals and had an entirely different idea, hooked his arm and together they transformed into Dorothy and the Scarecrow from *The Wizard of Oz*, skip-dancing across the lot as if it were the yellow brick road. Marc remembers laughing as they'd continued straight into the market, leaving him to field the stares and grumblings of disapproving townsfolk. He also remembers how they hadn't asked him to be the Tin Man, the Cowardly Lion or even Toto, and how he wished they had.

The couple downstairs returns to middle-age. Neither has gained any weight to speak of, and but for minor aesthetics, both simply look like older versions of themselves. One who knew them as teenagers would likely still recognize them even after all this time. Marc has not been so fortunate. Not only is he someone else now, he looks the part. His hair is so thin he's nearly bald, and his once bright brown eyes, saddled with heavy black bags, have faded considerably. In his thirties he gained thirty pounds, and his once-powerful build has turned slumped and soft, weakened and irreparably wounded.

He studies Brooke's face, the lines and contours, the sculpted girl-next-door beauty of it, and allows all the wonderful memories to flood his senses. Warmth rises from deep within him. He embraces it and holds tight, knowing even then it will slip free and become pain and sorrow, a blade slicing to the bone and carving away whatever shreds of dignity and security it finds, leaving a wake of blood and horror, regret and fury. Rage.

Spaulding finishes his wine, puts the glass on the coffee table and then casually leans down, scoops a hand under Brooke's ankles and swings her feet up into his lap. She pivots on the couch, facing him now and laughing lightly as he pulls her socks off and begins rubbing her feet. She sips her wine, throws her head back, closes her eyes and thanks him through a tired sigh. His response is evidently a witty one, as they both have a quick laugh before he resumes the massage. Long and thin, Spaulding's fingers engulf Brooke's diminutive feet, and as he works on them she seems to slip into something approaching true bliss. They both become quiet. The rain keeps on.

An odd buzzing fills Marc's ears. He looks to the

Gardens of Night

shadows a moment. Within the droning hum are consistencies ... patterns ... language. Suddenly, he envisions thousands of bees stacked one on top of the other, crawling about with instinctual, communal purpose, his skull their hive. There is something unnatural here, something that allows him to experience, feel and hear things he is not meant to know or understand in such a visceral manner. This thing inside him is nesting like those bees, preparing him for the arrival of something extraordinary and beyond human comprehension. He wishes the whales would talk to him again. He needs their sad, comforting cries, their spirit voices speaking in tongues.

As the buzzing fades, Marc remembers that night instead. He'd made reservations at a new Italian restaurant in town that had opened a few weeks before. Brooke was tired and didn't really want to go, but gave in because she knew Marc had been looking forward to it.

He remembers the picketers in town that night, passing them as he drove downtown and how they'd slowed up traffic. There had never been such a spectacle there before, but in the days preceding that night an organized group of protestors had converged on town, recruited many local citizens and gained considerable media attention. *Bay State Tech International*, a communications, manufacturing and engineering company that employed several hundred people, was one of the few companies in town and by far the largest. They had recently signed a contract with the Department of Defense, the details of which were said to be classified. But leaks to the media alleged the company was actually developing top secret equipment for The National Security Agency, and the more fevered the protests became, the wilder the stories grew. Claims ranged from the company being involved in everything from the production of computer chips designed to be implanted in unknowing human subjects, to mind control and psychological warfare experiments, to bombarding local citizens with bizarre sound waves, to the testing of extraterrestrial transmission technology.

He and Brooke had discussed it like everyone else in town, but had fallen firmly on the side that believed the company was more than likely simply doing something closer to what had been publicly claimed, which was the development of communications and satellite software for the military.

They'd touched on it briefly that evening over dinner, but conversation had quickly turned to happier things. Marc had the lasagna. Delicious initially, by the time they were on their way home it was sitting in the pit of his stomach like a bag of sand. He was so bloated he just wanted to get home, collapse on the couch and maybe watch television a while. He'd even joked about it. *"I feel like a townhouse with legs,"* he told her as they approached the house. *"I'm so ashamed."*

He could still hear Brooke's laughter.

There's a man in the driveway.

Even through the horror…

What's he doing?

The agony…

Just standing there.

The protestors…could one of them have become lost?

Who is it?

Or perhaps they'd taken to canvassing neighborhoods in the hope of recruiting more local support?

Not sure.

There were an awful lot of strangers in town that night…

※

Later, long after he has had his fill of memories and watching Brooke and Spaulding chat in the room below, her bare feet strategically left in his lap, moving slowly, subtly back and forth against his crotch, their heads back and eyes closed, pretending they are doing nothing other than quietly sitting together even when he casually releases his erection from his pants, Marc has tucked himself away in someone else's bed. He sees Brooke's silhouette cross the top of the stairs; hears her shed her clothing before she slips in next to him and spoons. She thinks he's asleep. Marc closes his eyes and believes it too. The softness and warmth of her body pulses against his back, washes over him as she snuggles closer. Her lips nuzzle his neck then she lays still, breath slow and steady as she drifts off to places where he can no longer follow.

There, in the dark, visions of the beautiful night nurse find him. Her gray snake tattoo comes to life, coils around her and constricts violently. Yet she responds as if touched by a lover, eyes rolled to white and mouth dropped open in ecstasy as others... two others... drift from the shadows behind her. But he cannot see their faces. Hidden beneath black shrouds, their heads bowed in what must be prayer, they reach for him with hands covered in wet soil.

Like they've just clawed their way from fresh graves, Marc thinks.

Noises downstairs interrupt, and the visions—or are they dreams, false memories sent to anger and frighten him?—burn and blister away like film stuck in a projector. Marc listens a moment, and just above Brooke's breathing hears Spaulding down in the kitchen, no doubt getting the woodstove going.

Rain drums the skylight. Marc looks up, meets its gaze.

There are no stars.

The night has gone blind.

Five

By morning the rain has stopped and the sun is out with promises of a bright, clear and beautiful day. Although Marc went to bed first, he is the last to get up. He awakens to the smell of freshly-brewed coffee, and as he staggers down from the loft and crosses into the kitchen he realizes Spaulding and Brooke have already showered and dressed. The woodstove is going strong, and unlike the night before, the chalet is filled with a stifling blanket of heat.

"Morning," Brooke says cheerily.

Spaulding smiles at him from the head of the table, a half-finished cup of coffee and a pack of cigarettes before him. He's one of the few people they know who still smokes, though he's a very light smoker—always has been—and is rarely actually *seen* indulging. "I know I said I'd quit," he says, realizing Marc has noticed them, "I just haven't gotten around to it yet. I keep hoping it'll come back in vogue, you know? Anyway, promised Scott there'd be no smoking inside so I've been sneaking out to the deck for a puff now and then. I was telling Brooke I was out there first thing this morning, watched the sun come up over the trees. Breathtaking, absolutely breathtaking."

Marc wishes he'd stop talking but keeps his thoughts to himself.

"We've got nada for breakfast," Brooke announces, "so we figured we'd get something out." She pours then hands Marc a cup of coffee and motions to the table, as if he's somehow forgotten it's there. "There's got to be a diner or restaurant or something along those lines in town somewhere."

"Besides," Spaulding says, "we need supplies, campers."

"It'll also give us a chance to poke around a bit," Brooke adds.

"From what Scott told me that should take all of about ten minutes. Apparently there are a few shops and whatnot but not much else. He said the few chalets and cabins out this way are mostly owned by out-of-towners who only visit periodically, and that the townies tend to be somewhat insular and keep to themselves. Not unfriendly particularly, just not the warmest folks either. He said he goes into town as little as possible."

Brooke frowns. "Well that sounds delightful."

"Yeah, Scott warned me that it's got a bit of a Deliverance-North vibe, but nothing too awful. Dasgar's just a little backwoods town, so don't expect the most heartfelt reception ever, that's all."

"Doesn't make any difference, we probably won't be going into town again anyway."

"You guys go ahead," Marc tells them. "I'm going to stay here."

Even before he's finished speaking he can feel the tension in the room rise. Spaulding and Brooke exchange troubled looks. "Honey," Brooke says, moving behind him and gently rubbing his shoulders, "won't you come with us?"

Spaulding takes his cue and stands. "Speaking of hideous addictions…" He pulls a jacket from the back of his chair, scoops up his cigarettes and heads out through the sliders to the deck. "Excuse me while I feed mine."

Brooke sits at the table. "Why don't you want to go?"

"I'm tired," he tells her, "want to take it easy. Wasn't that the whole point of coming here?"

"Yes, but—"

"Then you two go." He sips his coffee. "I'll hang here."

Brooke draws a breath and lets it out in a slow, shaky exhale. "Do you think it's a good idea for you to be here by yourself, though?"

"Oh, for Christ's sake." He slams his mug on the table, causing it and Brooke to jump. "I promise not to turn the stove on, play with fire or run with scissors while you're gone, OK?"

She stands and moves away. "Don't get angry."

"I'm not a child."

"I understand that."

"Then stop treating me like one."

She swallows so hard it's audible. "You need to calm down."

Marc realizes then that he's clenching his fists so tightly his arms have begun to tremble. He nods, opens his hands and lets his arms relax. "Sorry," he says softly. "I didn't mean to…"

"It's all right."

"I'm capable of taking care of myself, Brooke."

She looks at him, an eyebrow raised.

He retreats to his coffee and traces of his reflection in the inky pool. "You'll only be gone a couple hours, right?"

"I can't imagine it'd be much longer than that."

"Then I'll be all right. I promise."

Brooke returns to him, leans close and from behind, wraps her arms around his neck and kisses his cheek. "Be careful and don't go anywhere."

"Yes, Mommy." He reaches up, touches her hand and melts into her.

She unhooks her Blackberry from her belt and places it on the table next to him. "Spaulding's number is programmed in there on the call list," she explains. "If you need anything or whatever, just call and—"

"Sure, OK."

"Well, you know. I mean, if—"

"Brooke," he says, twisting in the chair so he can see her, "*OK.*"

Nodding, she runs a finger beneath her lower lash but fails to conceal the fact that her eyes are moist. Despite her carefully constructed façade, Brooke's wounds are still as dangerously close to the surface as his are, and the slightest provocation can drop her to her knees. "I'm sorry. It's just…"

"Yeah," Marc sighs, no longer able to face her. "I know."

Where are the whales? He wonders.

Speak to me…tell me your secrets…whisper them in my ear.

Have they fallen asleep? Have they died?

Free me. Heal me.

Or is he the one imprisoned in dreamscapes of the dead?

The familiar, the safe, the known, all of it has long-since evaporated. Yet alternate versions exist, taunting him with false gods and deceptive promises of salvation, deliverance from an infestation of demons well beyond redemption.

"I'll bring you some breakfast." Brooke pulls on her jacket and smiles, disguise back in place. "I love you."

He answers without looking up. "And I love you."

Once they've gone, in the quiet solitude of the chalet Marc remembers a dream from the night before. With the whales mute his sleep was visited by lesser gods, and though most of the minute detail escapes him he remembers that Brooke and Spaulding were living together in a tiny cottage in the woods. These woods. In the dream the cottage was actually the chalet, but looked nothing like it. Everything unfolded like a movie in Marc's head, playing out before him the way normal people dream, the way he'd dreamed before the night of the incident. A passive witness, he appeared nowhere in the dream. Perhaps he no longer existed. Perhaps he never had. He can't be sure. He seldom feels real anymore. All he knows is that Brooke and Spaulding were happy, and that the entire dream was seen as if through a filtered lens, like his eyes had been smeared with a thin film of clear liquid. A bit thicker than water or tears, it left everything slightly blurred, askew and just out of synch.

A while later, Marc finds himself in the shower, head bowed as hot water pounds across the back of his neck. The muscles there are tight and strained, and the pulsating water feels good. He braces himself, placing his hands flat against the back wall of the shower, and stays where he is for a very long time, countless thoughts, emotions and memories flooding his head.

When it's over, he remains in the shower despite the chill in the air. He watches the tiny droplets, fascinated by how they trickle down the walls to the drain below. It's not as if he's never seen this, perhaps he's just never paid such close attention. When he looks long enough, hard enough, the water drops turn black, like ink or blood from very deep within the body, and stain the world as only he can see. He reaches out, touches the shower wall with crimson fingers, and wipes it all away.

ಸುಂ

He is alone. Really alone, and lost in a new kind of quiet. Coupled with the newfound silence in his head, he notices other sounds as they slowly emerge from the hush… the cadence of his breath, occasional creaking noises as the chalet settles, and the crackle of wood burning in the cast iron woodstove. Marc looks through the sliders, beyond the deck to a pile of cut wood stacked neatly against the back of the chalet. He wonders who put it there and how long it took to cut and stack. He begins to count the pieces of wood as his mind searches for patterns and clues, listens for messages, but he catches himself and stops.

Marc grabs his jacket and ventures out through the sliders to the deck. There seems little reason to lock the doors, as the odds of someone coming to call or snooping around the chalet are nearly nonexistent. Still, he has learned that what appears to be safe or even unlikely seldom is. It is a lesson he's learned well, one he's learned by fire. So it is with defiance rather than indifference that he moves down the steps to the yard, stuffs his hands in his pockets and leaves the property unlocked while he goes for a walk.

The air is crisp and clean here, a bit cold but not too. It feels good in his lungs and makes his eyes tear. He pulls as much in as he can, taking one slow deep breath after another. At the back edge of the property, mere feet from where the forest resumes, he notices something he hadn't seen the night before, a small wooden shed. Closer inspection reveals that the door has been secured with a padlock. He

Gardens of Night

looks back at the chalet and the stack of wood. The ax must be in this shed, he thinks. Quickly, before he can think too much about it, he tells himself he can't imagine why that would be of any interest or concern to him. In answer, a chill slithers along his spine and laps the back of his neck. He knows better but blames the cold anyway, and with Brooke's voice running through his head, *"Be careful and don't go anywhere,"* Marc wanders into the woods.

The trees are enormous, living shadows looming over him he cannot be sure of. Looking up at them the way country bumpkins stare at skyscrapers in Manhattan, he studies their branches and tops and trunks like he's never seen trees before. In some ways, he never has.

At least not like this.

When he stumbles and nearly falls over an enormous gnarled root he returns his attention to the path, one which is old, narrow, and, he guesses, probably the result of long-term migrations of indigenous animals, as it's more subtle and natural to the setting than manmade paths tend to be. Funny, he thinks, how so many other animals can affect landscapes without altering basic aesthetics. Native Americans were able to live *with* the land, to exist alongside and in harmony with it. But for such rare exceptions, Man is consistently obvious, destructive and intrusive to the planet, a great trampling *thing* plodding across the Earth with total disregard for the balance of nature or even themselves. As Marc moves between the trees he tries his best to do so with grace and respect, listening to and absorbing as much of the world around him as he can. But while he would prefer to commune with nature, clear his mind and walk the woods alone, the past will not allow it. Following close behind, it clings to him, a long shadow skulking about with murderous resolve, a predator locked on the scent of its prey. And then the thoughts come so quickly. He tries to sort and listen to them—to *hear*—each and every one, but they crash into him with the shocking force of violent rapids and carry him away just as he realizes they've taken hold. Before he can scream for help he's already drowned, so Marc walks harder, faster, tries to focus on the beauty around him, the power and magnificence of it. Surely there are animals here too, hidden and watching. Forcing his way through the memories and horrors he tries to listen for them. Maybe that's it, he thinks. Maybe the universe hasn't stopped speaking to him. Maybe he's no longer listening. *Yes, it's all right there. I just have to hear it.*

Suddenly it feels like he's falling, toppled into a bottomless pit. *This must be what it's like to forget how to fly,* he thinks. The sensation of tumbling down grows worse as he plummets deeper and deeper, the victim of an endless freefall to nowhere, gaining momentum until the screech of air rushing through his ears becomes deafening and painful.

And then, silence.

Brooke's face arrives, emerges from the darkness. Her hair is mussed and her eyes are brimming with lies. She pretends to be all right but she's not. Marc can see it in her face, a face he knows well. He has traced every inch of it with his fingers, kissed every spot. And he knows those eyes and all that lies behind them even better. It is not a memory, not quite, but something similar.

With familiar hands she clutches his cock. Holding the shaft, she presses the head to her lips. As it enters her mouth she closes her eyes and suckles nosily. Some time later, it leaves her mouth with a loud pop and her eyes snap open, like she's been jarred from a deep sleep. "It's almost there," she says dreamily, "I can taste it."

Someone yanks him back, pins and holds him still with rough, powerful and calloused hands. Sour breath washes down over his face as eyes above him blaze with anger. A gravelly voice whispers so only he can hear. *"In the realm between this world and the underworld, at the roots of the tree, that's where they dwell."* And then those same hands have hold of what little hair he has left. They force him up so he can see Brooke. He's in her mouth again.

He cums. Blood.

It pours from his cock, escapes lips that even then are clamped onto his erection, runs down across him, splashes his belly and coats his skin, matting down hair and filling his navel as Brooke gags and tries to pull away. But she's held there by another set of hands, forced down deeper until her eyes roll to white and a slow trickle of blood seeps from her nostrils. Her blood mingles with Marc's, wets them both down in a rain of crimson, impossibly flowing from him even as he tries to kick and get free.

"Yggdrasil... it's dying..."

His body writhes about, convulsing as if hit by an electric shock. He can smell his flesh burning.

"Water and fire are the keys. They are life. They are passage."

Consumed by a sea of screams, the whispers die. The forest is all around him again, the world spinning and the trees threatening to crash down and crush him. But instead he simply stumbles into a clearing, leaned forward and moving so fast and with such force that he slaps the ground with a resounding belly-flop. His hands break his fall as best they can, but the ground is hard and coarse and scraps his palms like concrete might.

As he scrambles onto all-fours, he sees a small cottage.

In the center of a stone walkway leading to the front door stands a lone figure. "Who's there?" the figure—a woman?—asks. "What do you want? What are you doing on my property?"

Marc struggles to his feet. Lightheaded and confused, he paws spittle from his lips and looks around, trying to get his bearings. "I don't know."

The woman's thin gray hair is combed straight back from her forehead in a rather severe style, hooks behind her ears and stops just short of her shoulders. Dressed in black leather boots, a long black woolen coat with matching scarf wrapped around the neck, accentuating a jaw-line and a stoic face, flesh pale and eyes concealed behind large round sunglasses, the lenses black as coal, she looks like some displaced and aging fashion model from the 1960s. Sleek and thin to the point of appearing somewhat emaciated, she remains statue-still, arms hanging at her sides. One hand clutches a small revolver.

"I'm staying at a chalet not far from here," Marc explains. "I went for a walk in the woods and I…" His eyes go to the revolver and his bowels clench. He takes a wobbly step back. "I'm not well, I—I got confused, I'm sorry."

"Are you lost?" Her voice is less anxious now, nearly kind. "Is that it? You're lost?"

Please put the gun away, he thinks. *Don't make me take it from you.*

As if she'd read his mind the woman's posture relaxes and she saunters a bit closer, heels clacking stone. "I'm sorry about the pistol," she tells him. "But it's not every day a man I've never seen before comes running out of the woods like the hounds of Hell are on his tail and collapses in my yard. Not to mention that a woman alone in these parts—especially a woman like me—has to be careful."

"I didn't mean to frighten you."

"I'm not frightened."

"I'm just…"

"Lost?" she says again, a slight smile pursing her thin lips.

Marc nods. "Have I been here long?"

She doesn't answer right away. Perhaps she's gauging the sincerity of his question, but with her eyes hidden he cannot be sure. "I watched you a moment or two before I came out. I saw you fall, you went down awfully hard. Are you sure you aren't hurt?"

He halfheartedly inspects himself. "I'm not hurt."

"You said you weren't well."

He shrugs. "A bit dizzy."

"What's your name?"

"Marc."

"I'm Wilma. Wilma Malloy."

He forces a smile. They so seldom come effortlessly anymore. "I'm sorry, Ms. Malloy, I—"

"Wilma's fine. Can I call someone for you, Marc?"

"Call someone?"

"Surely you can't be out here all alone."

A sudden wind, cold and harsh, escapes the trees, rushes into the yard and slices through them both. In unison, they look to the forest.

"There's another storm coming." Wilma sighs. "Soon."

No, the whispers tell him. *It's already here.*

Six

 Marc steps from the car, ignoring his instincts, and moves toward the man in the driveway. He's still a good twenty or thirty feet away, and his face remains obscured by shadow as the setting sun behind him sinks lower in the sky. Marc is about to ask the man if he can help him with something when his cell phone begins to vibrate. Marc snatches the phone from his belt and glances at the display.
 ~Private Number~
 Though he normally would've ignored the call something tells him to answer it. He has the strange sense that being connected to another human being at that point might be a good idea. He holds a finger up, indicating he'll be with the man in a moment, and answers the phone. "Yes?"
 An empty hiss...
 "Hello?"
 The line clicks, dies.
 He holds the phone out and away from his body as if hopeful it might somehow explain itself. With a shrug he returns the phone to his belt and looks to the man in the driveway. He's moved closer, closed the gap between them, and has come into clearer view. His head is slightly bowed, and he appears to be staring at the driveway. "Hi," Marc says. "Can I help you?"

"*There is no fate,*" the man replies in monotone, "*that cannot be surmounted by scorn.*"

Baffled, Marc stops in his tracks. "*Excuse me?*" But even then, though he is not sure he heard the man correctly, or if in retrospect he even spoke at all, the words have purpose, meaning. He knows this, wants to question it—needs to question it—yet senses he understands in some primal way. He can't place it, but the phrase is vaguely familiar and summons emotions that are at once puzzling and terrifying. And it changes something in him. He feels it come awake. Alive…shifting… moving…

Something horrifying...

As the man raises his head, the shadows part to reveal his eyes and face, and it is then that Marc realizes he should've never gotten out of the car.

ಽಂಡಿ

The cottage is small but more spacious inside than he'd imagined. An old woodstove in the corner burns strong, filling the house with waves of stifling heat. Marc normally finds such levels of warmth oppressive, but here it generates a sense of comfort and reassurance, cradles him in the knowledge that he is safe within these walls. Decorated with curious combinations of country charm, ironic chic, and a series of furnishings one might expect to find in an upscale Manhattan apartment rather than a cottage in the woods of upstate New York, the main living area consists of a Parisian Style black table, scrollwork wrought iron corner shelves housing various trinkets and knickknacks, and a pair of comfortable chairs that bookend a matching loveseat. On the maple coffee table is a tattered copy of *The Myth of Sisyphus and Other Essays* by Albert Camus, and a pair of aged photographs in small standing frames. One features two little boys and a cat. The other is a posed group shot of a rather motley crew that looks to have been taken on a city street. A modest and nondescript rug covers much of the hardwood floor, and on the far side of the room a divider/dressing screen with an Asian motif stands open as if left there mistakenly. Along with the aroma of burning wood, a vague scent of potpourri hangs in the air, and the walls are adorned with numerous framed pieces of art, mostly abstracts mixed with a Warhol reproduction. One in particular catches Marc's eye, a poster-sized framed photograph of a woman decked out in a sequined ruby gown. Her makeup is heavy and she wears a large platinum wig. In her hand is a microphone and she appears to be singing. Despite the patent changes, and stage lights out of frame that paint her in a soft indigo hue, Marc realizes the woman is his hostess, the photograph presumably having captured her during an onstage performance of some kind several years ago.

He hovers about a while before sinking down onto the loveseat.

Moments later Wilma steps through a wall of hanging onyx beads in the doorway to the kitchen. She carries a quaint serving tray on which two cups of tea, a server of milk, a silver bowl full of sugar cubes, a miniature pair of tongs, two spoons, napkins and a small plate of shortbread biscuits have been placed, and sets it on the coffee table with a smile. Trailing seductively behind her is a black cat, its tail raised and yellow eyes watching him. "This is Mr. Tibbs," she explains, cocking her head toward the animal.

"Interesting name."

"My brother was a Poitier fan and, well, it's a long story. His name is sort of a tribute to my brother."

"Hello there," he says to the cat, who seems fascinated

by him but keeps his distance.

After handing Marc one cup Wilma takes the other for herself, adds a spot of milk and a sugar cube then moves to one of the chairs and sits. "For God's sake, don't stare so, Tibbs. It's rude."

Thoroughly apathetic, the cat slinks away, hops into the other chair and begins to bathe with manic repetition.

Coat and sunglasses removed, Wilma's figure is even thinner than Marc originally thought, and her eyes, while pretty and wise, also appear quite tired. This is a person who has lived life to the fullest, but the majority of that life is behind her. Despite what he suspects are her best efforts, Wilma's face has aged considerably from the one in the photograph, and rather than a sequined gown she instead sports black jeans and a black turtleneck, which along with her black leather boots contrast nicely with her silver hair and pale complexion.

The revolver is no longer in hand or on her person.

Marc wonders where it has gone.

"Well, it's certainly not every day that I invite strange men into my house," she'd told him while they were still outside, "but I usually have very good instincts when it comes to these things. I've found that the lost often have a way of attracting one another without even realizing it. Maybe it's synchronicity, maybe fate, who's to know? Why don't you come in and sit a while?"

"It's OK, you don't have to—"

"You'd never try to hurt me, would you, Marc?"

He stared into the black lenses. "No, ma'am, I wouldn't."

"You've been hurt quite deeply yourself, haven't you?"

Unsure of what to say or how to answer, he shrugged.

"Come in for a bit," she'd said, rescuing him. "Catch your breath and have something warm to drink. Then we'll see about getting hold of someone to come and fetch you. I don't know about you, but I could use some company and adult conversation for a change."

Marc sips his tea. It's weak but feels good on his throat. His palms, scraped from his fall, still ache but aren't bleeding, and the warmth from the cup soothes them. He remembers earlier times, when he was good at this kind of thing, when he could slide in and out of nearly any social situation with relative ease. Now negotiating even the simplest things have become insurmountably awkward. "Thank you," he says, raising his cup to her, "it's very good."

"Nice day for tea," Wilma says, crossing her legs at the knee. "So are you new to the area or renting?"

"My wife, an old friend and I are staying at a chalet not far from here. They went into town for breakfast and supplies."

"An enchanting experience for sure."

"I wasn't supposed to but I went for a walk while they were gone."

"Under house arrest, are we?"

Marc smiles softly, dutifully. "I have some issues."

"Don't we all?"

"It's all right, I—I mean, I'm not dangerous or anything, I just…"

Wilma points to the tray. "Have a cookie, love."

Marc takes one, nibbles it. "Thank you. You're very kind."

"I have my moments." Wilma gives him a wink. "Where are you from?"

"Massachusetts, near Cape Cod."

"Small world. And more synchronicity. I grew up not far from the cape myself. Spent quite a bit of time in Boston in the 80s too." She smiles but seems distracted by more serious matters. "I've lived in Greenwich Village for years now. Normally I'm not here this time of year, but I needed to get away for a while, was so hoping for some peace and quiet, and if nothing else, being out here certainly provides one that. I've always been a city girl, but I've come to appreciate this place. We—my partner Christopher and I—bought it several years ago as a getaway. We used to come every year for a few weeks in the summer months. He loved it here. This is the first time I've visited since…"

Quiet descends on them like the vulture it is.

"Chris died a few months back."

He somehow knows that there is more to it than that. This man did not die from a heart attack or cancer, but something else, something unexpected and avoidable, something pointless. Violent. There are indications in Wilma's demeanor, in her soul only someone like Marc can see and feel; a residue of evil unique to violence and those it scars.

"I'm sorry."

"Thank you. We were together a very long time. I miss him terribly." She sips more tea. "Horrible thing, but then death almost always is."

"Yes."

"You know something about that yourself, don't you?"

He nods.

For now, she leaves it at that. "This is the first time I've ever come here alone, actually."

"I shouldn't have intruded," Marc says, "I'm sorry, I—"

"Don't be silly. You're my invited guest. Besides, I've been out here all alone for days, puttering around this place and wallowing endlessly in my own sorrow. Isn't *that* cheery?" She takes a cookie from the tray. "Tibbs is a great friend, but he doesn't say much. It's nice to have someone to talk to."

Marc feels a connection to her, shared knowledge and

pain. This person has known violence and suffering well, and not in small amounts. They are kin.

She points to the Parisian table, and a framed photograph there of a dapper looking older man and herself, arm-in-arm. "That's Chris and me, taken just last year."

Marc studies the photograph a moment. "He looks like a nice man."

"He was."

"You look happy."

"Yes," she says, eyes glistening just for a moment.

"What happened, Wilma?" He wishes he could snatch the words from the air and return them to his mouth before she hears them, but it's too late. He sips his tea, avoids eye contact and finishes his cookie.

"Someone split his head open with a baseball bat," she says evenly.

Marc clenches shut his eyes, hiding from the man in the photograph and the blood and screams calling him.

"He was on his way home from the market late one afternoon when a group of young men in a car began harassing him. According to witnesses Chris tried to cross the street and get away from them, but they followed. They cut him off at the next corner—just a block from our apartment, can you imagine?—and one of them got out and beat him to death with a baseball bat. Right there, on the street." This time, when she brings the tea to her lips, her hand is trembling. Cup rattles against saucer. "Terrible things… fear, hatred, anger."

Not always, he thinks.

"And such a waste of a wonderfully kind and gentle man who on his worst day wouldn't have hurt a fly."

Marc feels the sadness churning, becoming rage. "And you?"

As if broken from a trance, Wilma adjusts her position

in the chair and asks, "What about me?"

"On your worst day, would you hurt a fly?"

She looks into Marc's eyes as if truly seeing them for the first time, but says nothing. Very slowly, a wry smile breaks across her face. "Hard to say."

"What happened to the men who did this?"

"They've yet to be caught. One witness got a partial license plate but it hasn't amounted to anything. The police are going through the motions but I suspect that's largely due to the political pressures and media attention. It's being considered a hate crime, of course, but I still don't think it's gotten the highest priority. Much as things get better out there, some things never change. In the end, who cares about some dead faggot?"

Marc opens his eyes. "I do."

In that moment he envies Wilma in ways he can never express and she will never realize. Even after such violence, she functions. She welcomes a stranger into her home. She trusts. She loves. She lives.

For Marc, there is no going back. His secrets—perhaps secrets no more in her presence—are webs he cannot escape, murderous vines he can never untangle, desperate and bloody hands clawing violently at him from below, pulling him back to flames that burn them all.

With twisted sounds lingering in his head, odd shrills of agony set to a backdrop of noise somewhere between the distant buzz of helicopter blades and the drone of heavy machinery, Marc scampers away, reciting mantras to calm himself, assurances and lies that everything will be all right if only he stays calm and breathes. His eyes lock on the coffee table, searches it for something, anything, to focus on.

Assuming he's turned his attention to the photographs there, Wilma motions to the one featuring a pair of young boys and says, "That's my little brother Dignon, our cat

Homer, and me. I was still pretending to be William then, as you can see."

And he does. Marc stares at the little boys and the cat in the photograph, and they save him, if only for the moment. There is melancholy in these two, this little boy she says is her brother and the other that was once her. The smiles are for the camera, mere deceptions etched onto impossibly young faces. Only the cat seems authentic, having already solved mysteries these boys will never fully decipher. Marc tries to recall pictures of his own life from that age but comes up empty. He knows they exist. He just can't quite drag them into the light. His youth was relatively happy and carefree, and he's certain such photographs would reveal a boy blissfully unaware of what was waiting for him in the years to come, someone for whom desperation and pain the likes of which Wilma and her brother were already experiencing at that age simply did not exist.

"Long time ago," Wilma sighs. "Dignon died when we were young. Not too long after that photograph was taken, actually. He was a wonderfully gifted storyteller, a lover of film and fiction and all things magical, mythical and romantic. He was a very special little boy, a prophet, and my best friend."

Marc doesn't know what to say, but he believes her.

"You remind me of him," Wilma tells him. "You don't look alike but you have a way about you, a similar aura, perhaps."

"Did violence take him too?"

"It took us both." She looks away, as if she's seen something pass by the window on the far wall. "We came from a very abusive home. Our mother died giving birth to Dignon, and our father was… he was a deeply disturbed man."

He wants to touch her just then, to put his hand in

hers, to squeeze them and tell her she's not alone. Instead, he sips more tea and nods thoughtfully.

"But my *God* what a charming host," she says. "Forgive all this doom and gloom, won't you? I'm just awful, grieving away in my woodland cottage and communing with the dead like some pitiful spinster in an old fairytale, how unspeakably morbid! "

Marc wonders about Brooke and Spaulding. Have they returned to the chalet yet to find him gone? Probably not, he's only been gone...how long *has* he been gone? It's as if time no longer exists here. And that's just fine. He motions to the poster. "You're a singer?"

"Oh hardly, love." She waves her free hand about as if to clear the air of foul odors. "I used to perform now and then in drag shows just for fun. And God help me, it *was* fun."

"I'll bet you were very good."

"You're sweet."

He returns her earlier wink. "I have my moments."

"Ha!" she barks with approval.

It feels good to laugh. He has laughed, hasn't he?

"What do you do?" Wilma asks, and then, realizing he didn't completely understand, adds, "For a living, I mean."

"I'm on medical leave right now but I manage an office supply store."

She considers this a moment. "That's not who you are, is it?"

"No."

"What were your dreams?"

Outside, the wind picks up. The cottage creaks.

"To be a writer, but that's gone now."

"Replaced by what?"

Screams... horror... blood...

"Nothing," he says. "It's not important, I—"

"I realize we've just met—and who knows, we may never see each other again—but it's all right to tell me. It's *safe* to tell me, do you understand? Here with Tibbs and me, you're among friends." She leans forward and pats his hand. "You're among friends."

"Something terrible happened to my wife and me," he admits. The words liberate him, if only temporarily, and he embraces the release. "Ever since I've had dreams I don't understand. Something's happening, something impossible."

"I've seen the impossible. I've touched it. There's no such thing." Wilma carefully places her cup and saucer on the table. "Much of life is myth, Marc, a fairytale full of wonderment and beauty, horror and fear, love and hate, pain and suffering, jealousy and greed, compassion and sacrifice. What we've lost, what we've forgotten, is that sometimes fairytales are true. Fate led you here to me so we could share this exact moment in time and draw from it what we will, what we must. Besides, can't very well have a fairytale without a fairy, now can you?"

Marc cannot remember the last time he has smiled like this. It feels delightfully foreign. "Maybe you're my Fairy Godmother."

"I'm as close as you're liable to get in this life, love."

The cottage is already rather dark, but outside the light has shifted. The world has grown suddenly darker, too dark for so early an hour. Perhaps fresh storm clouds have rolled in and blotted out the sun, casting the cottage in longer, deeper shadows. Mr. Tibbs raises his head, looks to the windows as if to be sure there's nothing more to it, and then fixes his stare on Marc.

You hear them too, don't you?

Marc feels himself nod, remembers the spider spinning its web in his hospital room.

They're just outside the door.

The back of his neck shivers, and a sharp pain stabs his temple then trickles down into his jaw.
Don't let them in.
Fear has become his god. He looks to the floor in worship.
With a resigned sigh, the cat resumes bathing.
"Tell me about your dreams," Wilma says.
"There's this old farmhouse." Marc swallows, realizes this is the first time he's told anyone. Is that why he's here, as she suggested? His hands have fallen asleep. "It's calling me, drawing me to it for some reason. I have this strange connection to it in an almost spiritual way. At first the farmhouse looks deserted. It's not, though. Someone... some *thing* lives there."
Wilma rests her chin in her palm. "There's quite a bit of farmland in these parts," she says. "Lots of old farmhouses, some still working, some abandoned long ago. Would you recognize the area, if you saw it again?"
He finally raises his eyes from the floor. "It's just a dream."
"Are you sure?"
He runs a tingling hand over his head. His scalp has begun to perspire.
"Are you afraid of this place?" she presses.
"It's a part of this somehow. These *things* I've had in my head since the night Brooke and I were... since that night."
"What kinds of things, love?"
"Voices. Feelings. Communications from..."
"From whom? From what?"
"I don't know."
She stays quiet a while. "You said something terrible happened to you and your wife."
He nods.

"And this brought about these changes in you?"

"Yes."

"I know a thing or two about violence. Chris died alone on a city street. My brother died in my arms in a cold and dark place, a horrible little space in our own private Hell. Violence changes us. It kills things in us, precious things. But sometimes it awakens things too. Maybe it awakened something in you."

"Like what? Madness?"

"Nietzsche once said, *'There is always some madness in love. But there is also always some reason in madness.'*"

"This has nothing to do with love."

"It has everything to do with it. Love binds and sets us free, damns and saves us all at once. And when these horrible things happen, love is all we have left, even if it's just the concept of love, the hope of love, the memory of love. I can see how troubled you are, Marc, how tormented you are by what's taken place, and while I don't know the specifics, I understand, believe me I do. These things in your head, maybe you shouldn't fight them quite so hard. Maybe you should let them speak to you and see what they have to say."

"What if they're lying?"

She smiles warmly. "What if they're not?"

Set against a pristine backdrop of ice and snow, visions of blood-red roses fixed with steely spikes rather than thorns drift through Marc's mind. "I think it's something evil," he tells her.

"It very well may be." Wilma scratches her cheek with a fingernail painted red as the roses. "But *evil*, at best, is a difficult term, better applied to the realm of religion than psychology."

Marc looks to her, half-expecting to see Doctor Berry sitting there instead.

"Were the men who attacked Chris evil?" she asks.

"Were the people who hurt you? Was my father? Maybe. It's all horribly cold and lonely, but is it *evil* or simply a base piece of human nature we can never hope to collectively evolve beyond?"

"It's a matter of survival."

"I agree. But remember, survival is a viciously ruthless enterprise."

"Unwarranted aggression isn't survival. Defending yourself against it is."

"But one could make the argument that evil is simply trying to survive as well." She picks another cookie from the tray, nearly takes a bite then thinks better of it. "My point is that whatever's trying to communicate with you could be evil or divine. But in the end, if it's your destiny, a necessary and inescapable journey ordained by fate, does it matter?"

Pay attention to the things you'll soon see.

With a quick side-glance in Marc's direction, Mr. Tibbs curls up for a nap and begins to purr.

"Interestingly enough, the book I'm reading ties into our discussion." Wilma scoops up the paperback from the coffee table and asks, "Have you read Camus?"

"Not a lot. I read *The Stranger* in high school."

"How apropos." She places the book in her lap. "This is a collection of his essays. Are you familiar with the mythology concerning Sisyphus?"

He searches his mind for answers. "Is he the one who had to keep pushing the rock up the hill for all eternity?"

She nods. "Sisyphus was damned to the underworld by the gods, where he was sentenced to pushing what was essentially a boulder up the side of a mountain until it had reached the summit. Once there, the rock would roll back down to the bottom, and he'd be forced to start again. Backbreaking labor was his punishment, pointless, hopeless and repetitive. He was damned for flaunting his passion-filled life, hating death and stealing the gods' secrets. Of course it's a delicious metaphor for the futility of life, of struggle and the torture of one's mind, body and soul that so often seems to make little to no sense. But rather than Sisyphus's ascent, what interested Camus specifically was his *de*scent. He writes that the most fascinating quality of the story is when the stone rolls back to the bottom of the mountain and Sisyphus walks down after it to begin again. Because it is during that walk back down the mountain, as he descends deeper into the underworld and the darkness the gods have chained him to, that Sisyphus contemplates his hell, realizes its ramifications consciously and pushes on. And it is then, Camus suggests, that Sisyphus conquers his own doom. Camus paints Sisyphus as a man for whom torment is eternal. But also as a man who through constant torture has become better and stronger than the rock. In this sense, Sisyphus transcends the horrors of his existence and becomes something of a hero. In his triumph over the rock, even while still shackled to rolling it up that mountain again and again, Sisyphus rips his fate from the hands of the gods and returns it to his own. One mustn't rail against the rock. One must embrace it and defy the torture, and in that contempt for one's fate—good or evil—ultimately *become* the rock. In that moment the rock is defeated and one is, in the truest sense of the word, free. As Camus so eloquently wrote: *'There is no fate that cannot be surmounted by scorn.'*"

Fear rises…

Listen to the things you'll soon hear.

Marc remembers those words. He could swear he heard them once before, spoken by the man in the driveway. And like then, they illicit things from deep inside him, things otherwise dormant. "I know that quote," he says, heart racing. "I… I know it."

"Synchronicity strikes again," Wilma says.

He responds with an algorithm of yearning, an excruciating hunger for understanding within his warren of hidden and unholy configurations, equations, and possibilities. In distant worlds, ancient temples crumble, the rubble falling through his tattered mind like a rain of crushed glass. And all the while the shrouded figures from his dreams watch silently, motionlessly, with the vigilant eyes of the damned. There will be no shelter, no sanctuary. Not yet. He realizes this now. His journey is preordained. Perhaps it always has been.

Like Sisyphus, he has little hope of escape, only the eventual triumph of enlightenment. He imagines himself in freefall, spiraling down gracefully into deep water, the whales singing to him as he glides toward the rusted and barnacle-laden gates of the underworld.

"Did you know your brother was going to die?" Marc asks suddenly.

"Yes. He put his head on my lap and I told him it was all right to sleep."

"Were you afraid?"

"Yes. But his fears had left him by then."

"Why should a little boy have to die like that?"

"Why do any of us have to suffer? Because God is a cruel and unloving monster, or is it through such things that we attain true enlightenment?" She shrugs. "We all have roles to play in this life, love. We all have purpose. And just as in life, we have those roles in death. They may not always be what we'd hope for or choose, but such things are not for us to decide. Or, perhaps they are. Perhaps we've chosen our own destinies for some greater purpose we can't yet remember. Some come to suffer, some to enlighten, some to lead, some to follow. *All* come to die. And it's right to struggle, to fight for one's life. The desire for survival is natural in nearly all living things. But so is death. Release. Surrender. It is, after all, all right to sleep."

Distant memories beckon him, flashes of choppy ocean waters...

"Look, I'm no sage," Wilma admits, "no fairy godmother. But here's what I know. Regardless of which mythology one subscribes to, the common thread that runs through most is that long ago the era of Man began and Earth became ours. Ever since, the gods have waited, knowing one day we'd make the necessary missteps that would allow them to take it all back. In our blackest moments, Marc, that's when they'll wrench it free if we don't hold on tight. Because it's in those moments our humanity dies. But only if we let it."

The crack of bone... the spray of blood... the cries of agony...

He will not submissively slip away to madness. Not yet. If this lunacy is to take him, it will not be without a fight. He will go out swinging.

"Well, there's something unexpected." Wilma rises from her chair, moves to the window and pulls the curtain back to let in more light. It has begun to snow. "Strange, the way the sky went dark, I thought we were in for more rain. It's a bit early for snow even in these parts." She turns from the window. "More tea?"

"I should be getting back."

"That's probably best. No telling how bad this is liable to get. My cell's in my bag." She heads back to the kitchen. "You can use it to call your wife and—"

"I can find my way." Marc retrieves his coat from the arm of the loveseat.

"You're sure?"

He offers his hand. She accepts. "Thank you," he says, "for everything."

"Well thank you for keeping me company a while."

They hold hands and eye contact for several seconds before letting go. In that moment, this woman, who used to be a boy, alone in her forest cottage with her cat and memories, the ghosts of lovers and brothers and the tarnished dreams of gods drowning in the sleep of the tormented, seems something more than wholly human. And yet her humanness is what makes her real, genuine rather than imagined. Like him, she is as much flesh, blood and bone as she is spirit, enigma and myth.

In the nearby woodstove, a log collapses with a crack and a hiss.

The fire shifts, grows stronger.

Wilma walks Marc to the door, opens it and gazes out at the snow falling between the trees. A cold breeze rushes in but she seems not to notice. "I hope you find the answers you need, and I hope they grant you peace." She smiles, with just a hint of mischievous glee. "Hans Christian Andersen said *'Every man's life is a fairy tale written by God's fingers.'* Maybe he was right, maybe not. Either way, just remember: enchanting as they may be, in fairytales the forests are *always* dark."

Seven

Marc moves through the trees in search of the path back to the chalet. Smoky plumes of breath roll from his nostrils and mouth, mixing with the swirl of snowflakes to form a strange cloud about his head. *Like a halo*, he thinks, *a halo of frozen, beautifully intricate little razors.*

"Don't let them fool you," Archie, his roommate in the hospital had always told him. A stout, middle-aged man who shuffled about in pajamas and scuffed slippers, scribbling in a tattered little notebook he never let out of his sight, he'd often spend hours sitting on the edge of his bed staring into space, brow knit and lips moving in silent conversation. Endlessly running a hand over his bald scalp, he'd pontificate about the numerous conspiracies he was certain were constantly being perpetrated against mankind. "They go around opening doors without knowing what's on the other side, see? And then they make us run on through, see? I know, because I used to open those doors. Now I'm just a guinea pig like the rest of you poor saps." Word on the unit was that Archie had once been a successful electrical engineer at one of the leading universities in the country, and had specialized in the study and application of electromagnetism, which he described as, "Along with gravity, the most important and powerful force in the universe."

Marc still isn't sure if there's any truth regarding Archie's alleged past, but there is no doubt that he's someone for whom the line between insanity and brilliance is wafer thin. Either way, it was common knowledge that Archie was a lifer. He'd been institutionalized since the early 1980s. He'd never be going home, and he knew it.

As Marc hurries through the cold woods, he remembers one morning when the meds had been handed out. Archie had studied the pills in his little paper cup like he always did, and then just before popping them smiled hopelessly at Marc and threw them back. "Chemical Apocalypse," he whispered. "That's all it is, see? All those pills and powders and shots and liquids on every TV channel, every magazine page, every billboard, in every medicine chest in every home, lining the cabinets of every hospital, *that's* how they're doing it. No tanks rolling down the streets, no martial law or prison camps, no alien invasions in metal ships. Just a chemical apocalypse, my friend, that's what it is. It's already started, see? They're going to take it all from us while we're medicated, fat, lazy, smug and ignorant. And you know why they'll get away with it? Because we'll give it to them, see? We *think* we're smart, above it all, too informed and clever to worry about such nonsense. Think again. The world's going to sleep. And that's when they get inside our heads and steal it all before we even know it's gone. Just like in here, who knows what they do to us while we're asleep? We're the fallen, see? It's all a test, an experiment gone wrong."

Even now—perhaps especially now—Marc can't help but wonder if the crazy bastard was right. After all, here he is lost in the woods and already the whispering has begun, the hushed voices reminding him that if he'd just get back to the chalet and take a pill or two, everything would be so much better. He'd be calm and relaxed, and while all that confusion might not completely go away, at least he'd no longer be quite so concerned about it. *Don't you want to be at peace? Don't you want your mind to quiet down and stop fighting you so?*

"Our minds are often tempests," Doctor Berry once told him. "And liars."

Focus, he tells himself. *Focus on the here and now, on what's right in front of you.* But the harder Marc concentrates on his surroundings the more the forest looks the same. It becomes increasingly difficult to distinguish where he is and where he's been, or hasn't been. The maze of trees seems endless. But for the sounds of his labored breath, it is so quiet here, empty and stark. He stops and looks up through the whirlwind of snowflakes.

There is something undeniably beautiful about the ominous.

Black jagged treetops stab the slate sky, and as he pans slowly along the horizon, an unnatural intrusion to the skyline perhaps fifty or sixty yards in the distance catches his attention. An old battered rooftop cross, sticking up above the trees. "A church," he whispers.

Unsure of why he feels so drawn to it, Marc hurries through the forest with newfound purpose nonetheless, keeping the cross in sight as he negotiates the uneven terrain. After a few moments he realizes it's a greater distance away than he'd originally suspected. Undaunted, he continues on until he reaches a clearing. Sweating profusely despite the plummeting temperature, he stumbles into the open, out of breath.

An old and obviously long-abandoned church stands before him. The white paint has faded and chipped, and the structure, neglected and left to the ravages of time and the elements, is rotting and decrepit to the point where it looks as if a good sound wind might collapse the entire structure.

In front of the church is what looks to have been a small parking area at one point, but the forest has slowly reclaimed it, leaving only a suggestion of what had once been. To the left of the church, the remains of a narrow winding road disappear into the cover of trees. It was once (and apparently still is) the only way in and out of here by car. More importantly, it provides him with an escape route, as eventually it must lead to something more closely resembling civilization.

As if controlled by unseen forces, the wind picks up, moving with apparent purpose through the clearing, across the church and into the forest beyond. Obedient branches sway and bounce at its command, and Marc feels his cheeks grow cold and tight. Squinting through the snow, he approaches the church cautiously. There are other sounds beneath the wind, *within* the wind, he's sure of it. Distant growl-like whispers call to him, and a faint rasp of wheezing breath gurgles, barely audible but real as the wind concealing it.

The gusts die slowly, and the forest returns to silence.

Through the blown-out front doorway of the church, Marc can almost hear the ghosts of parishioners singing hymns, a beautiful choir of heavenly voices drifting and echoing through the forest. *Just a Closer Walk with Thee*, he thinks.

He approaches what remains of the front steps and tries to remember the lyrics. *Just a closer walk with Thee...*

The wheezing becomes louder, accompanied by a low groaning sound.

Grant it, Jesus, is my plea...

Marc climbs the wide steps. Overgrown weeds traverse the landing and continue on inside, thousands of snakes tangled one about the next to form a living blanket that crunches beneath his feet.

Daily walking close to Thee... Let it be, dear Lord, let

it be...

Another groan, louder this time, seeps from the church. Gurgling and baritone, it is the lung and chest rattle of someone close to death.

I am weak but Thou art strong... Jesus, keep me from all wrong...

And yet, even as Marc moves through the ravaged doorway and into the dark and musty church, he knows there is a decidedly feminine quality to it.

I'll be satisfied as long as I walk...let me walk close to Thee...

Inside, old wooden pews line either side of an aisle that leads to the remains of an altar, and an enormous stained-glass window occupying nearly the entire back wall behind it.

Through this world of toil and snares, if I falter Lord, who cares?

Intricate spider webs hang from the ceiling corners, and he knows then he's being watched by their creators. But for the unseen, this place is long forgotten. No one has stepped foot inside this building in quite some time, he thinks, at least no one human.

Who with me my burden shares?

Partially rotted floorboards creak under Marc's weight as he ventures further inside. The light changes, shifts to darker shades amidst swathes of light stabbing through the holes and tears in the building. And at the rear, through the remnants of the stained-glass window, light filters through the various panes of colored glass, draping the altar and surrounding area in ethereal blue and red hues that seem just slightly beyond the realm of anything he's seen before.

None but Thee dear Lord... none but Thee...

He stops, feels his knees quake and his palms begin to sweat. There, in the far corner, to the left of the altar, a form

sits draped in a dark hooded shroud.
When my feeble life is over, time for me will be no more...
The wheezing grows stronger, and the figure stirs, as if only then cognizant of Marc's presence.
Guide me gently, safely over to Thy kingdom shore...
Marc shivers from cold and fear both, watches the figure as its head moves upward, causing the hood to shift and partially fall away to reveal the craggy face of an impossibly old woman. Tufts of white hair protrude from the sides of the hood, and she gathers the shroud tighter around her with arthritic, liver-spotted hands, the fingers gnarled and twisted as if broken, nails pale and bloodless.
... to Thy shore...
But it is the hag's eyes he cannot escape. Covered with a film of thick milky cataracts, they appear entirely white, as if everything else has been scraped away.

Thin chapped lips part to reveal a toothless mouth full of black rotten gums. Her head turns suddenly in Marc's direction, and she sniffs the air with a sagging hooked nose. In a gurgling voice, she says, "I can smell you."

He notices a large wooden cross that had once been affixed to the wall is now on the floor not far from her. It is stained with what looks like very dark blood. "Who are you?" Marc asks.

"Urd." A deep groan escapes her. Slowly, it becomes laughter. The evil, pitiless laughter of a butcher. A butcher not of flesh, but of souls. "The farther you think you've gotten from us, the closer you get."

Everything in his being tells him to turn and run, but he remains where he is, mesmerized. "What do you want with me?"

"*So* unholy," she says, licking her lips with a sickly gray tongue.

Things whisper to him from the shadows. The tiny web-spinners, they're trying to help him. But their messages remain just beyond reach. Marc wants to close his eyes but knows if he does the blood will be waiting. "Am I dreaming?"

"Of course," she gurgles. "Come closer, and I'll show you."

Marc takes a step back.

"Can you taste it? It's in the blood." The woman slowly raises her arms up and out to the side as if to summon a higher power. "Can you *taste* your destiny?"

Something vile and foul leaks from beneath the woman, spreads in a slowly growing brown puddle of filth across the floor. Pleased, she smiles, and a large shelled bug crawls from her mouth, scurries over her chin and drops free.

It hits the floor with a click as Marc's stomach turns and the acidic taste of partially digested tea and biscuits bubbles up into the back of his throat. The bug scuttles away, past the altar and a bevy of frayed and bloodstained voodoo dolls scattered at its base. Haphazardly sewn together and tossed into the center of a chalk circle of indecipherable symbols, they remain littered with pins and draped in the feathers and severed claws of slaughtered chickens. Nearby overturned bottles lay empty and broken, the mysterious potions they'd once housed as forgotten as the prayers of those who had worshiped within these walls so long ago, and those who have since come to desecrate, or perhaps cleanse it.

"Yggdrasil," the hag cackles. "It's dying. It needs you, Victim Soul."

Blocking his nostrils with his forearm, Marc moves back toward the door as the woman stares up at the tattered ceiling with blind eyes, lips moving as if in prayer. The nauseating wheezing and gurgling returns, worse than before, and she raises her arms again, reaching higher and forcing open her dark robe. Horrible things glide beneath her pale, mottled flesh, eel-like things that slither about rapidly before coiling and tightening along her ribcage with a sickening moist sound.

And as screams shatter his mind, Marc finds himself back in the forest, back in the snow, drifting through clouds of his own breath. Lying at the base of a large tree, he is suddenly aware of his surroundings, as if violently shaken from deep sleep.

He scrambles to his feet.

It is still snowing, but there's been virtually no accumulation.

He wipes his clothes off and looks around. Nothing seems familiar. He searches the forest.

Something moves through the trees in the distance. Barely visible, it darts through the forest at an alarming pace. Running… it's someone running parallel to his position… but at such a distance Marc cannot tell if it's male or female, only that whoever it may be is running from something and looking back every few seconds as if fearful that something is gaining on them.

The rumbling sound of an automobile erupts from somewhere behind him. Marc spins and realizes he can see a paved road through the section of forest in that direction, and an old pickup disappearing around a bend. He looks back to the deeper forest.

The runner is gone.

ℰℐℂℛ

As he walks along the side of the road, unsure of exactly where he's headed, Marc remembers the hospital walls and the hallways that, much like this lonely road, seemed to run on forever, so many hallways and corridors leading nowhere and everywhere, winding and disappearing around corners and into oceans of shadows. And the muted cries of those trapped within that terrible place, he remembers them too, doomed souls who, apart from hopeless flights of madness, will never know escape. He'd lived his entire life until that point never even considering the possibility of ending up in such a place. Yet, there he was.

And Doctor Berry, in her skirt suit, boots and frilly blouse, hair pulled back from her face and held in place with a shiny silver clip, she haunts his memory as well. She wields no tape recorders or pads of paper, and takes no notes in front of him—as if capable of committing to memory everything they discuss—just a warm smile and endearing eyes keenly watching him as she asks questions in soft, soothing tones.

What's the last thing you remember?
Night had come.
Tell me about that.
It was dark, and I couldn't tell where I was anymore.
Were you conscious?
I don't know.
Do you remember experiencing other stimuli? Sound, smell, etc.?
I only remember falling.
Falling?
It felt like I was falling. But I wasn't afraid. The fear was gone by then.
What did you feel, Marc?
Like something was there… down there, below me… something in the dark, just… waiting... watching me fall closer and closer to it…
Do you know what it was?

The end.
The end of what?
The end of me.

Marc follows a bend in the road, and for the first time since that morning, begins to feel the effects of the cold. The snow is changing, becoming wetter and gradually turning back to icy rain. Just ahead, a small shack of a house sits back in the woods not far from the road. The yard is littered with debris and trash and a few rusted automobile parts. Dilapidated and sporting a small, partially rotted out front porch, Marc would have assumed the house abandoned were it not for the two people watching him. They are so still at first they look like posed mannequins, but the closer he gets the clearer into focus they become. On the porch, a woman of perhaps sixty sits in an old rocking chair, a young boy—her grandson?—standing next to her. The woman is heavyset, her dark hair streaked with gray and pulled up into a bun, her face heavily lined and tired, the skin pockmarked. She wears a long dress and cumbersome shoes which seem wildly dated and better suited to a frontier woman of the past than a person assigned to the 21st Century. The little boy next to her is no more than ten, with piercing ice-blue eyes and a shock of curly blond hair. In short pants and a matching blouse, he looks like a backwoods version of Little Lord Fauntleroy.

Marc stops, watches them. Through the falling snow they seem almost magical, a vision from some other reality mistakenly slipping into view. They stare at him as if entranced, eyes boring straight through him. Damned, he thinks. They have the eyes of the damned. Cold… bloodless… dead…

Slowly, the little boy raises an arm, extends his finger and points at Marc. The woman rocks slowly in her chair. Old wood creaks.

It is then that Marc realizes their breath produces no clouds in the air.

Dizzy, he staggers back, brings his hands to either side of his head and looks for a place to fall. It feels as if his knees will buckle at any moment, but he somehow manages to remain upright as he spins away and stumbles back up the road.

The shriek of tires on wet pavement snaps him back from the precipice as a car suddenly appears before him. Slamming its brakes, it comes to a screeching halt just feet from where he's standing.

He looks back at the forest and the shack.

The woman and child remain, staring.

"Marc!"

Brooke's voice.

She and Spaulding are already out of the car, looking like frightened parents who have been frantically searching for their lost child. Brooke gets to him first, grabs him by the shoulders and inspects him. "Jesus, are you all right? Where the hell did you go? Why would you do this, I—didn't we discuss this? You promised you wouldn't leave the chalet! We've been looking for you for more than an hour! You scared us to death! "

"I'm fine," he tells her.

"You're not fine, you—"

"I went for a walk." He reaches out and tenderly cups the side of her face. "I'm OK, I just got lost."

Spaulding stands a few feet away, looking around awkwardly.

"You're all dirty, did you fall? Are you hurt?"

"Let's just go." Marc takes her hand and glances back at the shack.

Spaulding sees the woman and little boy too. "Inbred Central," he mutters, "party of two, your table is ready."

Ignoring him, Brooke slides an arm around Marc and starts him back toward the car. "Come on, we're getting soaked."

"Oh, you're no fun at all," Spaulding says, hands on his hips. "I bet once Skeeter and Coon get home there's gonna be a ho-down. I'm pretty sure we're talking square-dancing here, people."

Brooke shoots him a look.

Spaulding responds with his best shit-eating grin. "What, you don't want to party with Belle Starr and Damien from the fucking Omen? Seriously?"

After helping Marc into the backseat, Brooke closes the door, sealing him inside. He watches the sky through the window, barely cognizant of the voices outside. The snow is gone.

There is only rain.

Eight

There are moments, between the pain and flashes of violence, where Marc captures glimpses of the past with startling clarity. The colors are vivid, the details so crisp that they can only stem from a place just shy of reality. In those moments, he wonders about the greater power that sits watching, and why it does so with such passivity. Why can't it deliver and save him? Does it choose not to? Or is it simpler than that? Are such matters his charge, not God's?

Yggdrasil, it's dying. It needs you, Victim Soul.

He remembers it was summer, though he can't be certain which one. Last summer? Two summers ago? He'd watched from the kitchen window as Brooke pulled into the same paved driveway where later it would all begin. Back from an outing at the beach with some girlfriends, an afternoon drinking Coronas and sitting in the hot sun, she'd returned looking sated, relaxed, unencumbered. Her skin had tanned nicely that summer and was already a light bronze. Her hair was up and held in place with a clip, but it was disheveled, indicating she'd put it up either hastily or without paying particular care. Her sunglasses sat atop her head, and she was dressed in a white bikini top and a pair of khaki shorts that covered the bottoms. Barefoot, she climbed from the car, a beach bag over her shoulder. He'd sensed then there was something off about her, but before he could give it much thought Brooke came to an abrupt stop, as if she'd suddenly remembered something. She stood motionless a while then continued on toward the house. Due to the sun's glare he knew she couldn't see him in the window, so he watched quietly, the sounds of his wife's movements drifting through the screen like whispered secrets.

It wasn't until she came through the door and joined him in the kitchen that Marc realized Brooke had had far more to drink than he'd originally thought. She blinked rapidly as her eyes adjusted to the lower light in the house, put a hand up to her forehead like a lookout and said, "Hi. Why is it so dark in here?"

"Hi. It's not dark."

"Seems dark," she said, tossing her keys on the table and letting her bag slide from her shoulder onto the back of a kitchen chair. "Think I got a bit of a burn."

He watched as she reached up and gently rubbed the back of her neck, and it occurred to him that she still looked so young. In stores teenagers or twenty-somethings often referred to him as *sir*, which always made Marc feel old. He didn't feel like a *sir*, he felt like a contemporary. But they never did that to Brooke. She usually got *Miss*—despite the wedding band and diamond—or even better, no moniker at all, as if she were still an equal, a member of the in crowd who didn't need a title or the polite respect reserved for one's elders. *What we see*, he'd thought at the time, *is not always what's really there.*

It wasn't clear to him when or how this had happened. He had no memory of a single event or even a slow slide into such things. Instead it was as if one day the veil had been removed without his knowledge, revealing the truth behind it for the world to see. Unaware, he'd ventured forth, thinking it still in place. What had become of the cool and strength of his youth, the confidence and feelings of indestructibility? He still felt it, maybe even still believed it, but he'd become a paper tiger without even knowing it. He was a middle-aged married man working in an office supply store. Certainly nothing wrong with that, it was honest work for honest pay, but hardly the stuff of cutting edge cool. He was a good man, a good husband, a good worker. Wasn't he? Brooke wasn't so different, really. She was a married, middle-aged teacher, for God's sake, how had she managed to retain her sense of self and convince the world of its continued relevance? He wasn't jealous, just unable to understand why he'd been so completely severed from those things. Had he done it himself? Had he given them up as a means of survival—necessity—in an environment where such traits couldn't continue to exist, much less thrive? Or had he been robbed while sleepwalking through life, his essence stolen the way everything else would be stolen in the months to come? And if so, who was the thief?

Fate... Destiny...

And then, in an instant, standing in their kitchen, for the first time Marc had begun to wonder if he was losing Brooke too. Her body was one most women half her age would've killed for. Her stomach was still flat and tight, sexy, her legs shapely and taut. If anything, she'd improved with age.

He wasn't entirely sure what he felt in that moment. A bit of annoyance at how long she'd been gone, the condition she'd come home in and the outfit she'd been gallivanting around in, perhaps. Yet, she looked so sexy and beguiling he couldn't be angry with anyone but himself for his own weakness when it came to her.

It was hardly the end of the world or an enormous issue, but he couldn't help but notice how the white bikini top was still damp and left nothing to the imagination. She may as well have been topless for what little it managed to conceal. Next he focused on the soles of her feet as she strolled across the kitchen to the adjacent bathroom. Black as tar. Odd, if she'd merely walked from the beach to her car and from her car to the house. He trailed behind, stopped in the open doorway and leaned against the casing as Brooke let her shorts drop to the floor, stepped out of them then peeled down her bikini bottoms and lowered herself onto the toilet. "Had a bit to drink, huh?" he asked, feeling more like her father than her husband.

As she began to pee she chuckled softly. "You think?"

"Probably shouldn't have been driving."

"Oh, I'm fine," she said, waving him off dismissively. "God, lighten up."

The wilder, rebellious side of Brooke was one he had seldom seen outside of controlled situations of which he was part. But on that day she'd drifted off into behavior that had apparently awakened her wilder side without him, and that was something new. Still, he'd thought, it was just a day at the beach with some girlfriends, maybe he was overreacting.

"Noticed you got the lawn mowed," she said. "Looks nice."

"Yeah, thanks, I—Brooke is everything all right?"

She wiped, stood up, and rather than pulling her bottoms back on, pushed them the rest of the way off and kicked them aside. "Of course," she said, yanking back the shower curtain. "Why?"

He'd never before suspected infidelity, and didn't feel this warranted such concerns, but clearly something was out of kilter with his wife and he needed to find out what it was. "You just don't seem like yourself."

"I had a bit more to drink than I should have and sat out in the hot sun all day, made me a little goofy. It's no big deal, Marc." She turned on the water, pulled the clip from her hair and placed it on the sink. "Let me shower, then we can do dinner. There's hamburger in the fridge. Feel like firing up the grill?"

He nodded; watching as she removed her top and stepped into the shower. Looking back at him, she smiled. Beautiful as it was, there was something different about it, something forced. Like a vampire running from the light and hoping to hide until the metamorphosis was complete, Brooke was slowly returning to her usual self but not quite there yet. Still grinning, she pulled the curtain closed then peeked out at him. "Or you could always get in here with me and we'll worry about dinner later."

Despite his attraction and love for her, what he remembers so clearly is how his body and mind absorbed the pain of that moment. His pain. And hers.

When he stepped into the shower and wrapped his arms around his wife, he noticed the black staining the bottoms of Brooke's feet had begun to wash free, swirl and flow to the drain like ink. It was as if some diseased and decayed part of her was escaping, fleeing her body.

Now, when Marc remembers that day, he knows it was something else. Not a part of her but rather a foreign body, a parasite fleeing the scene and taking with it unspoken fears, the curse of complacency and the shelter of alternate personas from separate realities.

Are any of us exactly the same when no one, or someone else, is looking?

Later, after everything had happened, there had been a few brief quiet moments amidst the chaos. One moment in particular comes to him whenever he remembers that summer afternoon: the first time he and Brooke had been alone in the house together since he'd returned from the hospital. It was a remarkably quiet afternoon, bright but cloudy. He'd stood before one of the bedroom windows, watching the street.

She remained in the bedroom doorway, wringing her hands and trying, he was sure, to think of something—anything—to say. There had been talk of moving, of course, of how returning there was not healthy for either of them. But they couldn't simply pick up and leave. They had a mortgage, responsibilities. Brooke had spoken with a real estate agent but nothing had been settled. There were simply parts of the house they no longer went to. Closed doors and sealed areas to be ignored and never spoken of.

Marc knew the woman from that summer day was dead, murdered right before his eyes. And as phantoms spoke to him, filling his head with things he could not yet comprehend, he was left to guess at what still remained, and to question how much of who they'd been before was real.

"Were you happy?" he asked.

When she gave no answer he'd turned from the window. Brooke stood in the doorway, her face unusually drawn and pale.

"Before," he pressed, "were you happy?"

She answered quietly, her voice a whisper. "Weren't you?"

෨෬

The car barrels along the rural road, heading directly into waves of darkness. Within moments night has enveloped them and the rain has evolved into a full-blown storm. Thunder rolls, and in the distance, enormous bolts of lightning crackle and split the sky in brilliant bursts of blue and white.

"Christ," Spaulding mutters. He switches the wipers to high but it doesn't help. "An infestation of locusts and we'll pretty much have the whole Biblical Apocalyptic weather thing covered."

"You don't believe in any of that," Brooke reminds him. "Remember?"

"Thus my amazing wit in relation to the topic."

"Slow down a little," she says, looking back at Marc nervously before returning her attention to what little of the road she can see. "The last thing we need is an accident out there."

"I've got this," Spaulding tells her, though he does slow the car a bit.

Marc remains quiet amidst the storm, huddled in the backseat with his nightmares of Dr. Berry and the hospital. His eyes roll to white.

Tell me about the strange people you saw the other night, Marc.

I don't think they were people.

As in not human?

Not sure. They were covered in dark clothing and hoods.

If they weren't human what were they?

I don't know. They almost looked like…nuns.

Nuns are human.

Yes, but they weren't like any nuns I've seen before. Not…exactly…

Were you dreaming?

I was wide awake.

Sometimes we have waking dreams.

This is something else.

But you're not sure what?

No.

Had you ever seen them before?

Never.

And have you seen them since?

No.

Where were you when you did see them?
The rec room, just before nightfall. They were on the edge of the grounds.
Did anyone else notice them there?
Not sure. I don't...I don't think so.
Did they try to communicate with you in any way?
They didn't have to.
What were they doing?
Just standing there...watching...
What do you suppose they wanted?
Me.

"We don't want to miss that turn off for the chalet or we're liable to spend hours on these back roads," Spaulding says, his voice snatching Marc back. "They all look alike."

Marc's eyes slide open as lightning explodes up ahead, illuminating the night just long enough for him to see the same hooded figures in black standing in the forest on either side of them. He closes his eyes and is met by visions of two plump black spiders tangled together in battle. The violence is instinctual, primal, void of conscience. Pure. Even as they kill each other, Marc hears their messages ringing in his head.

Blood consecrates... fire and water, passage...

His hands clench to fists. Something's coming. He can feel its fear.

Suddenly Brooke screams. A large dark blur vaults across the windshield, its form cutting the headlights just long enough to reveal a flash of fur and hooves.

"Holy shit!" Spaulding jerks the wheel as Brooke screams again, this time bracing her arms against the dash as the car spins out. "What the hell was that?"

Tires screech above the din of thunder and rain, and the world whirls, an out-of-control carnival ride as the car skids sideways along the pavement, headlights knifing through darkness in arcing slashes.

Spaulding struggles with the wheel and pins the breaks. He is fast enough to prevent them from slamming into the oncoming trees, but too late to stop the car from falling into a ditch between road and forest, finally jerking to a stop and coming to rest at an angle. The violence of the stop slams his head into the window. As the safety glass cracks and smashes, Brooke ducks away, reflexively shielding her face with her hands. But she too is thrown from her seat and crashes into Spaulding, who flops up into an upright position, his face sprayed with rain and wounds that have already begun to bleed and bruise.

The last thing Marc sees as he flies across the backseat toward the driver's side door is his unconscious wife falling back into her seat, her body lifeless as a ragdoll.

In the murky fog he descends into, Marc sees himself watching the night through the window. Somewhere beyond his range of sight, the deer that ran in front of the car is now safely on the far side of the road and hidden in the dark forest. It stops, looks back at the car. Marc nods to the animal and it turns and lopes away. It has done what was asked of it. Or perhaps, as with so much else, the deer is not at all what it appears to be.

A single whispered word drifts through the night and finds him.

Verdandi.

And then, in stillness, there is only a driving rain assaulting the roof, the sound of labored breath, and the slow approach of several hooded figures, their black robes barely discernable in the darkness.

Nine

Although he doesn't yet fully comprehend why, Marc now realizes getting out of the car was a horrible mistake. "I'm sorry," he tells the man in his driveway, "what did you say?"

The man continues to stare at him, his towering form dark, sinister and draped in closing shadows. At closer range he appears to be in his late forties or early fifties. Gray stubble dots his chin and pockmarked face. "Didn't say a word," he answers; voice raspy, part whisper, part snarl.

Marc smiles involuntarily and shuffles about as an excuse to glance behind him at the car. Another man, this one shorter, wider and considerably younger appears, stepping through the shrubbery on the far side of the driveway. There is something in one of his mitt-like hands but Marc cannot see what it is. Heart hammering his chest, for a brief second Marc's eyes meet Brooke's, who is turned in her seat and watching him, still unaware that another man has moved in behind them. "Well," Marc says, stepping back and to the side so he can keep both men in his sights, "what is it I can do for you guys?"

Brooke, he thinks, lock the door. Lock the door, baby, lock the door.

"You can gimme that ring of keys for a start," the big

one says.

It takes Marc a moment to sort through the mounting uneasiness and confusion before he realizes what the man's talking about. His keys are in his hand but he has no memory of having taken them with him when he got out of the car. Instinctually, and without looking at them, his fingers feel for the longest key they can find. He pushes it to the front, holding it nonchalantly between his knuckles like a weapon. "Look, what's this all about? Who are you? What do you want?"

An odd but familiar sound to his left…

Marc looks quickly. The stout man has opened the car door and is motioning for Brooke to get out. Marc starts toward the car but in his peripheral vision sees the bigger man moving with him. He stops, not wanting these men any closer to them than they already are. The man halts with him and again Marc turns a bit so he can see everyone. "Get away from her," he snaps, pointing to himself while holding the squat man's gaze. "Deal with me, leave her out of this. Now what the hell's going on?"

The short one steps back from the car so Brooke can get out, motioning at her with the thing in his hand. Is it a gun? She immediately looks to Marc, her confusion giving way to terror. She speaks his name, he's certain of it, but he barely hears her.

"It's OK," Marc says, unsure if he's speaking to Brooke, the men, himself or all three. Robbery, he thinks, they're here to rob us. Yes, but he has no idea what these men have truly come to take. This sort of thing doesn't happen in their quiet little town. They must be escaped convicts or drug addicts desperate for a fix, something along those lines, he thinks. "What is it you want, the car?"

The younger man laughs. It is a depraved and unpleasant sound that causes Brooke to take a step away from him,

Gardens of Night

arms folded over her chest, face barely able to contain her fear. As she moves, even though she's several feet away, he catches a whiff of her cologne. Marc reaches a hand out to her, signaling her to come to his side, but the man puts a hand on her shoulder. She squirms away and out from under it as Marc again moves toward them. "Hey, keep your fucking hands off her."

It is then that he realizes the thing in the man's hand is, in fact, a gun, some sort of semi-automatic pistol. He's certain now, because it is leveled and pointed directly at him. Marc has never had a gun pointed at him before and the reality of what it could do to him at such close range is sobering and horrifyingly real. This isn't a movie or a television show, some mindless shoot-'em-up he can watch from the safety of his couch. He raises his hands awkwardly.

"Put your hands down," the tall one says.

Marc does. "We don't want any trouble with you guys," he tells them. "This doesn't need to get out of hand. You want the car, take it. We don't have a lot of cash but you can have whatever we've got. We have a few credit cards too. Take them." He holds the key ring out for him, a peace offering. "OK?"

"We want something we'll take it. Don't need your permission."

Marc forces himself to look back into the big man's diseased eyes. Something passes between them in that moment but he can't be sure exactly what it is. He pulls the phone from his belt and tries to dial 911, but in one quick motion, the younger man steps forward, swats the phone from his hand then jams the gun against Marc's chest with enough force to knock the air from him. "Who you think you're calling, you fucking faggot?"

As pain shoots through his ribs, Brooke again tries to get to him. The man stops her a second time, clamping a beefy hand on her shoulder before she can take more than a step. With a resigned look that can only be helplessness, she doesn't even try to break free of him this time, but instead looks to the ground, her shoulders slumping forward in what she now understands is defeat.

The older man slowly reaches out and takes Marc's keys from him. "We're going in the house now, all of us. Understand?"

Marc looks around frantically. Where the hell are the neighbors? How can this be happening right out in the open without anyone seeing? If he were alone he could simply run for it, but he can't leave Brooke behind so flight isn't even an option. His only choices are to comply or fight. If he complies, they might still get out of this alive. If he fights, surely one or both of them could be seriously hurt or even killed. Then again, these men are not new to this sort of thing, he can tell. There is a good chance both have killed people before, and once inside the house he and Brooke will be completely at their mercy.

"We're not going anywhere," he says evenly.

"Listen real good, boy." The older man gives a quick side-glance to his partner. "You move your ass and do like I tell you. Less you want your pretty little cunt's blood all over your nice driveway."

Marc's mind races. How did this all happen so quickly? He can still taste remnants from their meal. Just moments ago they were living a normal life, coming home from dinner. And then, suddenly, evil has found them. He looks over to his wife. With a demented grin the man deliberately presses the gun hard and deep into the side of Brooke's breast. She closes her eyes but says nothing. Would he really shoot her if he fights back? Marc can't take the chance.

He submits with a slow nod. His entire body trembles.

Together, all four move toward the house.

They have already begun to die.

࿇

He is alone. He realizes this quickly. There, in the dark. Jammed between the floor and the back of the front seats, Marc struggles to free himself. Once in a sitting position, he runs his hands over his face to make sure everything is still intact. A small trickle of dried blood stains the space between his nostrils and upper lip. He licks it, tastes the saltiness of the blood then wipes it away with the back of his hand. Lightheaded and nauseous, he lays back a moment and tries to collect himself. It is then that he hears something more than a relentless rain pounding the roof. An annoying dinging sound pulses all around him. The front doors are open, and the dashboard lights cast everything in an otherworldly glow.

The car is still running.

Spaulding and Brooke are gone. Only Brooke's purse remains, most of the contents spilled across the seat and floor.

Marc draws a few deep breaths and waits for his head to stop spinning. Once it does the nausea retreats as well, and he pushes himself up and over the seat and yanks the key from the ignition. The car dies, silencing the dinging, and he returns to the backseat, pushes open the back door and tumbles out.

Breaking his fall with his hands, his palms hit pavement and the pain reminds him of how he'd scraped them earlier. Locking his arms, he drags his legs from the car and falls to his knees on the side of the road. The darkness has grown so deep and the storm so violent that but for the occasional

lightning strikes, visibility is only a few feet. He calls out to them but no one answers.
Move. You have to move. Find them.
Marc gets to his feet and staggers into the road. If there are any clues as to where Brooke and Spaulding have gone or been taken to, the night and rain conceals them, so he steadies his nerves as best he can and listens. There are living things within these woods that will help him, that can tell him what to do.
Nothing.
Memories of the deer return to him. Rainwater splashes and runs over him like blood. He wipes his eyes, tries to remember where the animal was when it crossed the road. Closing on what he suspects is the closest point, Marc crosses into the forest then breaks into a run once he clears the first band of trees. He has no idea where he is but somehow knows he's heading in the right direction. He can feel it. Though the forest is dense he negotiates it as if he's been there a dozen times before, avoiding branches and pitfalls with surprising grace he hadn't realized he even possessed.
He continues on for what seems an eternity, running through the forest, chest heaving, lungs burning, the world dark and blurry and wet, swaying and spinning as strange cries and murmured whispers emanate from the cradle of night encircling him. Without slowing his stride Marc looks right then left. He is not alone in the dark wood. With each blink of lightning, others emerge from the darkness. Running parallel to his position, their pale faces pierce the night and glow through the downpour. But they are unconcerned with him, each trapped in a prison of his or her own separate Hell. Instead, they growl like a pack of wild animals, possessed souls all, their desperation the ravenous terror of the forsaken. As Marc presses on, snapping twigs and

crushing leaves with each step, he does his best to ignore the infestation of massive trees looming overhead, and his mind locks on the singular, instinctual purpose of survival. Moments later, winded and finally slowing his pace, he realizes he is again alone in the enormous expanse of forest, a sacrificial lamb left for the gods of wind, rain, thunder, lightning, and death to do with what they will.

And then, quite suddenly, Marc emerges from the forest and finds himself at the edge of an open field. Drenched, he stumbles to a stop in order to catch his breath. Lightning rips the sky, revealing a considerable hill in the distance, the ghostly silhouette of a large gnarled tree standing atop it. And though he cannot see it, Marc knows an old farmhouse lies beyond that hill.

His bad dreams have come true. Again.

He breaks across the field and the rain falls even harder, as if to repel him. Though the terrain is pitted, he runs at full speed, certain his newfound strength, wind and energy is only adrenaline, but will do the job nonetheless. The night tilts and shakes with each heavy step, the rain pounding against his skin with such force it stings on contact. Great spears of lightning continue to crackle across the sky, and though they are frightening and Marc feels terribly vulnerable out in the open, he is grateful. Without the seconds of illumination the lightning provides, he'd surely become lost in the darkness.

As he reaches the far end of the field far faster than he thought possible, he scurries up the side of the hill, pitched forward to maintain his balance and pushing off with each long stride. Sisyphus sans boulder, he reaches the summit quickly and finally comes to a stop, wipes the rain from his eyes as best he can and waits for the next lightning strike. In the meantime he turns to the large tree. He's close enough now to be able to make out much of it through the darkness and elements. Up close the tree is enormous, with a fat trunk and lengthy, contorted branches. Lungs burning with each breath, he moves closer.

Lightning blinks.

Something in the tree moves. Something large.

Marc steps back, evil seeping from the tree like heat from a fire. A snake is coiled around a nearby branch, its body thick and massive, forked tongue flicking about as if it were an independent creature, black eyes invisible in the darkness but for their strange glistening. Had it not moved, slightly tightening around the branch upon Marc's approach, it would've remained undetected.

He listens, but the snake has nothing to tell him.

Thunder growls. Marc steps away and notices three old-fashioned wooden wells not far from the tree. Within seconds another bolt of lightning slashes the heavens, and there, in the distance, is the farmhouse and an old barn, exactly as he'd seen them in his nightmares. Sparse candlelight fills two windows in front, but otherwise the house is dark and quiet. To the right of the house is a small stone building situated a hundred or more feet away, off by itself. The squat structure looks like a place where tools and things of that nature might be stored, but could also provide good cover while allowing for a closer look at the farmhouse.

As the world returns to darkness Marc sprints down the hill, taking an angle slightly out of line with the farmhouse that should put him directly in the path of the stone building. He reaches it quickly, drenched, shivering and for the first time, aware of the chill in the air, the coldness of the rain. Falling against the back wall, his mouth falls open as he gasps for breath, chest heaving.

The few windows on the stone building are fitted with rusted bars, and the only door is a flimsy, ill-fitting, partially rotted wooden board, barely secure and precariously rattling with each gust of wind and spray of rain. He tries to open it and with limited effort wrenches it free and slips inside.

Marc closes the door behind him and sinks down to his knees. The floor is dirt and largely covered with hay. The building is very small, no larger than a standard tool shed, but it's so dark inside he can't make out much. Horrid smells of human waste, urine and perspiration fill the air, but as best he can tell, the building appears to be empty. He scrambles over to a lone window on the far wall that faces the farmhouse, stands and grips the cold bars like a prisoner. Squinting through the night, he watches the house a while, and but for the candlelight in the windows, sees no indication of life. Turning his back to the wall, he wipes his face and slowly slides down onto his backside, exhausted and doing his best to think clearly. He has to find a way inside the farmhouse. He has no doubt that Brooke and Spaulding are somewhere within those walls.

Something stirs in the corner to his right.

"Ain't no use hiding," a raspy male voice tells him from the darkness. "They already know you're here."

Ten

A match strikes, hisses and flares. Before Marc can figure his next move, the flame is touched to the base of a small lamp and light punches a hole in the darkness. The match dies, and the lamplight, though dim, is sufficient to divulge the source of the voice, an older man with a head of wavy silver hair and a matching unruly beard. His heavily-lined skin is bronze and leathery from hours spent outdoors, and his eyes, a dull blue that had probably once been quite striking, are glazed, bloodshot, and bear the sins and witness of a man who has seen and experienced a great deal, little of it pleasant. Even in sparse light, he appears filthy, as if he hasn't bathed in weeks, and possesses a smell that confirms it. The man places the lamp next to him, the light revealing a makeshift straw bed against the far wall, a threadbare blanket and a bucket Marc can only assume is used for waste.

He rises to his feet. The man is short but compact, dressed in grubby clothes. He goes to the crude door and pushes on it, making sure it's properly closed. "Careful," he says, "you'll let the night in."

With the barred but open windows Marc fails to see the logic, but lets it go.

The man scurries back into his corner and sits.

"Who are you?" Marc asks, still shivering from the

cold rain.

"I'm nobody. Kind of a caretaker for the place, you could say."

"You *live* out here?"

He chuckles humorlessly, lungs rattling. "Ain't been *alive* in a long time."

"What is this place?"

"The beginning. The middle. The end."

Marc gets up on his knees. "Two people, a man and a woman, my wife and a friend, they—"

"Inside." He motions to the farmhouse with his chin.

"They're here? You're sure?"

"I helped get them in the house."

"Are they hurt?"

"You need to ask them that. Pretty bad accident, though."

"Are they in danger here?"

"We're all in danger here."

"What about the police or—"

"Don't you know where you are?" The man picks something from his beard and looks at Marc the way one considers the simplistic naïveté of a child.

Lightning blinks. "Who else is in there?"

"The sisters," he says, looking away. "And the *sisters*."

"No more riddles, old man." Marc moves closer, ignoring a sudden wave of lightheadedness. "Please, I need your help."

Shadows play across the man's weathered face as he watches the rain through the window. "Nothing's forever. Even the sisters got an end."

"How long have you been here?"

"Don't know." Wind whips through the open windows, rattles the door. "Time's not the same here. It's never the same, not when we're like this."

"Like what?"

The old man gives a brown-toothed smile but offers no answer.

"I'm not asking again," Marc says. "What is this place?"

Sensing aggression, the man's smile slowly fades. "Wasn't always a farmhouse," he explains. "The land, the air, all of it had to be desecrated first."

"Why desecrated?"

"Only way the three sisters could settle here. They used to be someplace else, lots of places all over the world. For centuries, understand? And if it don't end here, they'll wind up somewhere else, pulling their strings." He motions to the farmhouse. "That was built on top of an old convent. Way back in the early 1800s, this was a place of God, or so they say. A cloistered order lived out here more or less alone for years. But then the area started to get more populated, and the questions started. The sisters claimed to be a holy order but nobody knew where they came from, who they were or what they were doing out here. Way the story goes the church didn't recognize them, labeled them heretics. In them days that's all the locals needed. They burned the place to the ground and butchered every last one of them nuns… or whatever they were. Fools had no idea what they were ushering in."

Marc's visions of nuns being burned at the stake and nailed to crosses by men in dated clothing, floods his memory. "I dreamed this," he mutters.

"Now the *other* sisters—the three—live here."

"Who are they?"

"You already know. You dreamed of them too."

A chill dances along the back of Marc's neck. Thunder rolls.

The man leans back, further into shadow. "The only things left from the convent are the catacombs. They still use them, underground passages that run all through here. That's where you got to go, the catacombs."

"Is it just the three of them in there?" Marc asks.

"Nah, they live there with the *other* sisters."

"The nuns?"

"They ain't regular nuns." He grins. "Wear their crosses upside down."

They weren't like any nuns I've seen before.

"But you said they were put to death, destroyed hundreds of years ago."

The old man nods.

Marc crawls over to the window, stands and looks out through the storm. The rain is still coming down in buckets, thunder still rumbles overhead and the wind has grown stronger, but the lightning strikes are fewer and farther between. The candlelight filling the farmhouse windows is barely visible. "How do I get in?"

"Knock on the door," the man says. "They'll answer. Devil always does."

With a questioning look, he glances back at the old man.

"Told you, they already know you're here. Fate always knows."

"They're waiting for me, is that it?"

"You heard their call." Hidden in shadow, only the man's bloodshot eyes breach the darkness. "That's why you're here."

"But what do they want with me? Why me?"

"It's your destiny…and theirs." As the man settles deeper into the corner he vanishes from sight. The darkness has swallowed him whole. "Later, you'll set me free. You got to… got to set me free. Promise you'll set me free."

Marc barely hears him, and without answering, stands and pulls open the door. The night rushes in as a cold and violent rain sprays his face. The murmur of hidden things slink through the night, but this time he's almost certain it's just the old man whispering to him from the darkness.

"Bring the hell, boy. Bring the hell."

※

Through the rain, a man. A dream, a Victim Soul emerging from darkness. Moving purposefully, he emerges from night and strides through the muddy open area between stone building and farmhouse, oblivious to the storm raging around him. As if a child of this turmoil, he closes on the house with the gait of a predator tracking prey and follows the narrow stone path to the front door.

Something moves past one of the windows, briefly interrupting the yellow glow of candlelight. As the rain pours down, night coils around him like the living thing it is, invades his senses, the world dark, alive, wet, dripping, moving.

Knock on the door.

He hits the sturdy but scarred wooden door with his fist three times, each knock harder than the last.

They'll answer.

A rattling sound cuts the night, most likely locks disengaging.

Devil always does.

The door opens. Slowly. From within, candlelight seeps out into the night, blurred by a relentless rain. And in the slim opening, a pale face. A young round female face with flawless skin framed in heavy black linen. Beautiful green

Gardens of Night

eyes blink at him innocently as her lips part into a bright smile.

Hardly the demon he'd expected.

The forests in fairytales, enchanting as they may be, are always dark.

"Who are you?" Marc asks.

"Sarah," she answers in a singsong voice. She appears to be barely out of her teens. "They told me you'd come. Another lost soul in the storm."

Marc nods, the rain running off him in torrents.

"Come in out of the rain," she says, stepping away from the door to reveal her nun's habit. The cross she wears is large, made of wood and hangs down to the middle of her petite torso. It is not inverted as the old man suggested. "It's all right," she assures him. "Come."

He hesitates, tries to see deeper into the house behind her. "My wife…"

"She's here, asleep of course."

As the young nun opens the door wider still, Marc steps through.

The interior of the farmhouse doesn't match the exterior, and he's surprised to find himself standing in a large, rather formal front room that smells vaguely of cinnamon and burning wood. Candles glow in ornate holders positioned strategically throughout the room, thick gold curtains hang open in the windows, classic paintings fill the walls in bulky wooden frames, and the furniture—chairs, a sofa and various end tables—are all wildly dated, as is everything else. It's as if Marc has crossed over into the 19th Century. He identifies the aroma of burning wood as flames crackle in a fireplace on the far wall, the room shielded from fire by a freestanding mesh screen positioned in front of a stone hearth. But the cinnamon smell remains a mystery. He moves about awkwardly for a moment, not entirely sure where or how to stand, his wet shoes squeaking on the hardwood floor.

"Why don't you sit by the fire and warm yourself," Sarah says, motioning to the fireplace. "Are you hungry? Would you like some hot food or a warm drink?"

"Where's my wife?" he asks, looking around nervously.

"She's safe," Sarah tells him through another smile. "Would you—"

"Listen to me, *sister*—or whatever the hell you are—I need to see my wife right now, do you understand?" He wipes the rain from his face with the back of his sleeve. It's so much warmer here, he thinks, somewhat stifling. In fact, is it rain he's wiped away, or perspiration? "And my friend, I—"

"He took a nasty bump on the head, but he's going to be just fine," she assures him pleasantly. "He and your wife are both resting quietly."

"Fine, then take me to them."

But for the sounds of their voices and the occasional snap of the fire, the farmhouse seems oddly quiet. On cue, heavy rain sprays the windows and a booming crack of thunder explodes overhead. Marc tries to see behind the nun to a narrow hallway just off the front room. She looks behind her, as if to see what he's looking at, then turns back to him with a benign but puzzled expression.

The heat quickly becomes overpowering. Marc sweats profusely, and the lightheadedness he experienced earlier returns. He feels sick to his stomach as well. Does he need his medication? Is this simply another of his anxiety attacks? Or is there something more here, something purposeful causing this reaction in him? Either way, he's running out of time, and knows it. "I need you to take me to Brooke and Spaulding," he says evenly. "*Now.*"

Sarah watches him, her irritating smile still in place. "First, you must rest."

The universe has fallen silent. Marc hears only trivial sounds anyone else would in such a setting. Has he been abandoned? Or is nothing else here truly alive?

"Listen to me," he says, or tries to say, his mouth thick, tongue heavy. Suddenly the room tilts like a carnival ride. He reaches for something to grab hold of but it's too late. His legs buckle and the floor rushes up to greet him.

Just before darkness claims him, a voice—one he's heard before in the desperate madness and lonely isolation of his hospital room—speaks.

The night nurse...

"Take him down," her sultry voice commands. "Take him down to the catacombs."

Eleven

He remembers waves of dizziness washing over him again and again and then a deep and frightening silence. The chilling silence of the grave. He imagines shaking his head to clear it but has no real sense of physical self, like he's suspended and dangling helplessly between consciousness and dreams.

Then I'm dreaming, is that it? Is it that simple?

No, because there's motion. Motion he can feel. His world is moving, rocking and bobbing as if he's lying atop a raft in open water. His eyes open. Above him, endless blue sky… but in the distance storm clouds are gathering, black and evil and full of hate. He sees, hears—feels—the ocean around him. He can smell it as a gentle breeze filters past and he struggles up into a sitting position. Not a raft but a small, time and weather-ravaged boat.

And he is not alone.

An older man, hunched and obviously suffering from some sort of degenerative spinal disease, stands in the rear of the skiff, steering and paddling a battered wooden oar with gnarled hands. Dressed in a dark hooded cloak, his features are craggy and one eye is covered with a black leather patch. The other, bloodshot and dark, is distended, causing it to bulge abnormally, as if the eyeball might pop

Gardens of Night

free of the socket at any moment. The man's nose is hooked and sagging with age, his mouth thin-lipped and speckled with tiny scars.

Marc looks to the horizon. They are headed directly into the coming storm.

"Where are we going?" he asks.

The man's only response is a crooked, toothless smile. But there is no humor behind it, only hatred the likes of which Marc has experienced only once before...in himself.

Marc feels tired—drugged—and is unable to shake it. He tries to get to his feet but can't. His heart is racing and the smell of the ocean is overpowering. Yet somewhere nearby there is safety, there is God. The whales...

He closes his eyes. Their songs come to him, sadly beautiful, and like him, chained to realities they can never escape. No one, no *thing* is free.

Sleep, they tell him. *Sleep, Victim Soul.*

And he does.

Later, he awakes. The boat has come ashore and lies in wet sand. The shrouded man is gone, his old oar lying in the back of the boat. Marc rolls onto his hands and knees then struggles to his feet. The wind has picked up, night has crept closer and the storm clouds have grown stronger, blackening the sky as they roll in over the heavens. But for a pair of tattered denim shorts, he is nude. Shivering, he climbs out of the boat and stumbles along until he reaches dry sand. The tall grass on a nearby dune catches his attention as it dances in the wind. He looks around. The beach is deserted. Or so it seems.

The whale songs are mere whispers now, legends at the edge of his consciousness, drifting in and out, in synch with the rhythm of ocean lapping shoreline. Marc trudges up a slight embankment to the dune, his feet sinking in the soft sand. The mounting sea winds push him along.

There, in the tall grass, on hands and knees, is Brooke, wearing a startling red bikini he didn't know she had. She frantically buries scraps of bloody clothing and other items in the sand, working furiously and looking back over her shoulder every few seconds. It isn't until he is nearly upon her that Marc realizes that it is body parts she is burying—severed arms and legs, hands and feet—and by her own feet, a human head caked in blood and bile, eyes gouged out, mouth frozen in a twisted grimace of agony.

He stops, tries to look away but cannot. Instead his eyes fill then spill free with tears as he retreats, nearly falling as he slides back down the side of the dune toward the ocean. "Stop," he whispers, barely able to see her now through the swaying grass. "*Stop* it."

Swept into a cyclone of madness, he runs for the ocean.

"It's all an experiment," a hollow, disembodied voice tells him. "That's what you are, what this life is, this world and the hideous things Man endures. It's all a celestial experiment gone horribly wrong. And someone has to absorb the sin and pain so that others might survive. You, Marcus. *You.* Find joy in the suffering, as the prophets did, as all Victim Souls do. Embrace transcendence through violence, cleansing through bloodshed. You've chosen this path, Marcus, it belongs to you."

He'd been running for the ocean… hadn't he?

Inside now, where it's warm and quiet, he is led by Brooke across a candlelit room to a bed, her arm around his waist as she guides him. He can feel her bare flesh against his, damp and sprinkled with tiny grains of beach sand, the coarseness tickling his skin. "Sleep," she whispers. "You need to sleep."

"We have to get out of here," he says, voice garbled. *Why do I sound like that, why—why can't I speak without slurring?* "What have they done to me?"

She lays him down on the bed and although he doesn't want to, he obeys submissively, allowing her to position him there on his back lifelessly. "What you need is a good night's sleep, Marc. Sleep now, OK?"

Brooke takes off his shorts, leaving him nude and exposed on the bed.

"Why—*don't*—why are you taking my clothes off?"

"You'll be more comfortable this way."

I don't want to be here I want to leave, where—where are my clothes—why can't I move, I want to get up why can't I get up I—Brooke, you—that's—that's not Brooke, that's not my wife—what are you, what—you're not my wife you're not my wife!

He realizes then that the bikini he thought she was wearing is in fact painted on…in blood…

She smiles seductively, running her fingers through the blood, smearing it across the rest of her body. "Yggdrasil," she pants, "it's dying. It needs you, Victim Soul. Water and fire are the keys. They are life. They are passage."

This is a nightmare, I—I'm dreaming—this isn't real, that's not Brooke, I—

Something moves in the corner. Marc's head lolls to the side.

Two eyeless men, whose souls have become forever entwined with his, stand in shadows. They're bleeding, their faces battered and horribly misshapen.

"Absorb the sin," she whispers, head thrown back in ecstasy as her hands move furiously between her legs. "Assume the pain, the suffering and the sin. So others might live, swallow it all and spit back wrath. *Be* the hammer of fate."

Back on the sand, Marc walks toward the ocean on an otherwise calm and bright moonlit night. There is no chaos, not anymore, as he stops near the waterline, removes his clothes and looks up at the stars. In their brilliance, he remembers earlier days, long ago but never forgotten; sees the beauty, the love and wonder in the breathtaking eyes of the woman he loves, the way she looked at him with such uninhibited hope and joy whenever they danced and held each other tight. Be it in a formal setting or just playing, it never mattered, the feeling was the same. What he wouldn't give to see that look in Brooke's eyes just once more. But even in dreams, even in the torment of his devastated soul, he knows it will never happen. They are moments captured in time, like photographs, something relegated to the past that one can see but never truly replicate again. It is dead. Gone. Murdered.

Through the blur of tears he gazes out at the ocean.

If Brooke were with me, he thinks, *she'd hold my hand right now, and together, we'd go swimming. We'd cling to each other, and looking into each other's eyes, let the waves carry us from shore. Nothing else would matter... only this moment... only us... because we'd be safe in each other's love.*

But not this time, my love. Sleep.

※※※

Marc comes awake in a small room. His first visions are of a ceiling cracked and stained with watermarks. The residue of nightmare clings to him with good reason, as he lies on a similar (if not the same) bed in the same small candlelit room found in his dream. Only this time he is alone. He rolls from the bed, feet finding floor as his head clears and his surroundings come into clearer focus.

A mild headache has settled in his temples, his clothes

are still damp from rain and perspiration, his scraped palms throb with pain and his entire body aches, but he seems otherwise unharmed. Except for the bed and a small table against one wall where a candle burns in an antique holder, the room is barren, with a low ceiling, a cement floor and close, empty walls that create a boxlike, claustrophobic feel. There is only one way in or out, through a heavy wooden door on the far wall. Marc rushes to it, tries to push then pull it open but the door has been locked from the outside.

Frantically, he smashes at it with the flat of his hand, ignoring the spikes of pain shooting through his palm with each blow. "Let me out of here!" he screams, his voice unusually hoarse and deep. "Goddamn it! Let me out! "

Several minutes come and go before he hears movement beyond the door, followed by the sound of someone throwing back a deadbolt.

Unsure of what's coming, Marc looks around the room for something—anything—he might use as a weapon, and chooses the candle. Scooping it up he holds it out in front of him at the ready as the door swings open with a loud creak. Through the flame, he sees Sarah in the doorway holding a tray on which a wooden bowl of thick stew sits steaming.

"You're awake," she says with a pleasant smile. "How are you feeling?"

"What did you do to me?"

"You're exhausted, you need rest." She raises the tray as if to remind him she's holding it. "I've got some hot food for you and—"

"I don't want your food!" he snaps. "Where's my wife?"

Sarah blinks at him innocently, her pale skin flushed in embarrassment. "I wish you wouldn't raise your voice like that. I'm only trying to help you."

"No, you're not." He moves out of the way and motions

for her to come into the room. As she does, he steps into the doorway and takes a quick peek down the dimly lit hallway, which is actually a stone tunnel of sorts, arched and dark, the floor tightly-packed dirt. He turns back to the nun. "Put that down."

She places the tray on the small table and backs away, hands held down in front of her, fingers entwined.

"Where am I?"

"The catacombs."

"Below the farmhouse?"

She nods.

"Who are you?" He moves closer.

"Sister Sarah."

"This is no longer a convent," he reminds her. "The old man outside told me it hasn't been in years. So I'm going to ask you again, *sister*, who are you?"

Her lovely green eyes watch him cautiously. "Some of us are still here."

"From the order?"

"Yes."

"How many?"

"Thirteen, including myself… but… I'm usually kept apart from the others."

"Why?"

"I'm not like them."

"What are they like?"

She answers in whisper. "Evil."

"And you're not?"

Looking as if his accusation has mortally wounded her, Sarah shakes her head in the negative.

"If the nuns here were slaughtered decades ago," Marc asks, subtly pushing the candle closer to her, "how is any of this possible?"

"Nearly anything is possible here."

"And the *other* sisters here? The three?"

"Urd... Verdandi... Skuld... fate... necessity... being..."

"Who are they?"

"The past... the present... the future." She bows her head as if in sudden prayer. "We serve them."

"You and the rest of the remaining nuns?"

"Yes. As do all living things."

"Nuns are supposed to serve God."

She raises her eyes. "They *are* God."

A shudder quakes through him. The candle wavers, casting shadows along the wall. "What do they want with me?"

She motions for him to close the door and then raises a finger to her lips.

Marc does as she asks, then stands with his back against it.

"Yggdrasil, it's dying."

He raises a questioning eyebrow.

"The large tree you saw outside near the wells, it's dying. It has many names in many different cultures, and has grown in the soil of nearly every corner of the globe. It is the literal Tree of Life, and if it dies, everything else dies with it."

"Including the three sisters?"

"All living things. Nothing is truly immortal. Everything has an end. But they can slow it down and prevent its death for now, through the water they draw from those wells. The liquid is magical. It stops the decay. But the wells are nearly dry, and as the fate of living things draws nearer, they must cleanse the darkness that draws us all toward death. They need a Victim Soul. A devout person chosen by God to absorb the pain and suffering of others, the Victim Soul accepts his or her role selflessly so that others might live. They need a Victim Soul now more than ever. They need you."

"Devout in the religious sense?"

"Not necessarily, just someone devoted to their efforts... and God's."

"I'm not devoted to God's efforts."

"You are. You just don't realize it."

"I'm not a holy man." The candle begins to shake in his grasp. "I've experienced horribly violent things."

"God is violence, Marcus. His angels are violence. Violence is simply the expression of His wrath. In that devotion to your task, *your* violence, you absorb your sins and the sins of others. You become their suffering, through the violence inflicted by you, others, Man and God. And in that suffering you find transcendence... deliverance not only for yourself but others. You become the hammer of fate."

"No," he says, emotion strangling him. "God is love. I—we—are violence. *Man* is violence."

"Do you see? Even in your suffering, your faith lives and you serve Him."

"The Three Sisters... what do they want to do to me?"

She looks to the floor.

"Sarah, tell me. What, exactly, do they need from me?"

"All that is inside you."

"I can't survive it, can I," he asks, though it's not truly a question.

"No," she says softly. "The blood in your veins is the blood of a martyr."

"This is fucking madness," he says, choking back equal parts sorrow and rage. "I'm completely insane. That's it, isn't it?"

"One has nothing to do with the other."

With his free hand, Marc angrily wipes the tears from his eyes. "Where the hell's my wife? Where's Brooke? Where's Spaulding?"

"I can take you to them, but we have to be careful." He thrusts the flame at her. "Do it."

Reluctantly, Sarah takes the candle, and with a slight nod, leads him into the labyrinth of catacombs.

Twelve

 And then, God. Dreaming. Like His creation Nero, the emperor who had countless subjects executed, including his own mother, and fiddled while Rome burned, He sleeps while Man wreaks havoc. But unlike Nero, neither neglect nor tyranny is the culprit. Instead, it is love. His is the weary sleep of an exhausted parent, the slumber of escape, of hope that when He awakens all He has created will finally understand what has been set before them. And while he sleeps, the rats run. Unseen things come alive; the magic of vanquished gods return and the world becomes fairytale, myth, a landscape of mayhem and martyrs, saints and sinners. All of it true and all of it lies. Everything, he thinks, and nothing…
 Innocence is dead. Faith is a ghost. The past is a lie, the present a trick of shadow and fog, the future a whispered promise never fulfilled. And through it all, the nightmares remain. Even when the horrors of torment are shattered by the fires of so-called righteousness, burned to ash and scattered to the winds of time, misery survives, anger lives, and blood runs red, drowning the world in the iniquity of Man. In the midst of such bedlam and carnage, no help arrives. We must save ourselves, he realizes, because in this life we're on our own. And in the absence of God, suffering

is illusion, pain is meaningless, love is irrelevant. There is only survival and the purity of its wrath.

The rest is blood, fire, water, passage. But to where?

The moment they enter the house and the door closes behind them, Marc knows they're doomed. He tries to lie to himself, to convince himself there's still a way out, but he knows there isn't. No one speaks as the strangers gawk and rubberneck as if they've entered a palace rather than a modest home. The stout one laughs excitedly, like the scenario is even more than he'd hoped for, while the older man gives Marc a sudden and violent push that sends him stumbling forward and into the table.

"For God's sake," Brooke says breathlessly. They are the first words she's spoken since this all began. "This isn't necessary, you..."

Marc meets her frightened eyes with a gaze of his own that silently conveys she needs to stay quiet. There's no telling what may or may not set these men off.

"Where's the bedroom?" the big man asks.

Marc straightens his stance. "Upstairs. Why?"

He looks to his cohort. "It's either that or the basement."

The younger man waves the gun around like a flunky in a gangster movie, finally leveling it on Marc. "Get your ass down the basement, bitch."

Marc knows if he leads them to the cellar he and Brooke will never get out of there alive. He has to risk lying. "The house doesn't have a full basement," he explains, "just a four-foot high crawlspace."

"Fuck it then." He motions to the adjacent room, a small den. "Let's just do it there."

The other one considers this a moment then nods. "Close them curtains."

Marc's heart sinks as the man with the gun does just that. He considers rushing the older man, but even if he manages to disable him, his partner is the one with the gun. He'll never make it.

"Get on in there," the older man tells them, pawing at the gray stubble dotting his scarred skin. "Do it."

As the curtains are yanked closed and the shades drawn, the light diminishes in the room, casting much of it into deep shadow. Displeased, the younger man nonchalantly switches on a lamp. A chill cuts Marc to the bone. Simple executions can be conducted in the dark. Apparently whatever these men have in store for them requires sufficient light.

Later, a door will be installed to close this room off from the kitchen and the rest of the house. Neither he nor Brooke will step foot in it again, but for now the small and suddenly cramped room remains open, easily accessed and flowing freely into the rest of the house.

Marc looks to the windows, wanting—needing—to see the outside, the street and the other houses, his neighbors, the world. But there is nothing. The world has come down to four people and a gun. Not so very far away are others who would surely help if only he could reach or signal them somehow. But it no longer matters. They may as well be miles away. He and Brooke exist in a void now, a separate hell.

When he thinks of this, it is mostly sadness he remembers. Horribly crippling sadness. Somewhere along the line they all fell in one way or another. They all died—or soon would—and wound up there, in this place, in this moment.

"What's happening?" Brooke asks once they're all herded into the den. "What do you want?"

From behind him, the older man draws a knife, presumably from his belt, that seems to materialize from thin air. Some sort of military commando style knife, it sports a ridiculously enormous blade. Holding it up with the ease of someone familiar and schooled in its use, he stares at the blade with admiration, clearly aware of what this weapon is capable of in his deft hands. He grins with an expression that should look silly on a man his age but comes off as unsettling and creepy instead. Oddly, there is a hint of joy on his face. "Ever seen one that big, honey?" The short man snorts through hideous laughter as his cohort slowly brings the knife to Brooke's lips. She shudders but accommodates him as he slides the tip of the blade into her mouth. "You like that shit?"

"Leave her alone," Marc snaps, but before he can step between them the stout man swings the gun at him. With a disturbing clang, it connects with the side of his head, sending a spike of pain across his temple and through his skull. He grunts, stumbles back and brings a hand to his face.

Marc sinks to his knees, and Brooke makes a whimpering sound but remains still as the man removes the blade from her mouth and drops it down to her throat. "Do that again and I'll carve her tongue out and make you eat it."

The pain makes everything real, turns fear to terror.

Marc struggles to his feet. A trickle of blood runs from his hairline down along the side of his face. The room tilts then corrects itself. Brooke looks to him but he has nothing for her, no saving grace, and they both know it. "This has gone far enough," he says groggily. "This—"

"You think we're playing games with you, bitch?" The younger man lumbers forward and jams the gun in Marc's face, roughly pressing the barrel into his eye socket. "Shut the fuck up!"

Marc's bowels clench, certain the man is about to kill him. The barrel is cold but smooth against his flesh. The room spins again. *Christ Jesus,* he thinks.

"Do the fuck," the older man says.

"Don't!" Brooke says suddenly, in a surprisingly

strong voice. "He—we're sorry. We're sorry, OK?" To illustrate her willingness to cooperate she raises her hands like Marc did in the driveway.

The big man turns to his gun-toting partner, and with his free hand, points at Marc. "This asshole says one more word or makes any kind of move—and I mean any *kind of move*—you shoot him in the head."

The short one laughs, taking the gun from Marc's eye and leveling it at his bloody temple. "Boom, motherfucker! Boom!"

The older man grins at Brooke. "Take your clothes off."

Marc watches helplessly, heart smashing his chest.

His wife's eyes assume a sudden steeliness he's never witnessed in her before, and without ever breaking eye contact with the man holding the knife, Brooke steps out of the black flats she's wearing, slowly unbuttons her blouse, pulls it off over her shoulders and drops it to the floor. She then hitches her thumbs beneath the elastic waistband of her ankle-length skirt, pulls it down, and, bending one knee and then the other, steps out of it and tosses it to the floor alongside her shirt.

The younger man gives a perverted laugh. His partner watches silently.

Resolute eyes still locked on the man's, Brooke unhooks her bra, arches her shoulders forward and lets it fall free of her breasts. Rather than catch it, she allows it to fall to the floor with the rest.

Marc closes his eyes. For Christ's sake, he thinks, do something. But the blow to the temple has left his equilibrium off, and no matter how hard he tries, he can't seem to stop the room from moving or his legs from feeling like they're about to give out.

When he opens his eyes again Brooke has already

removed her panties and added them to the pile of discarded clothes. Standing before them, she never wavers, cries, breaks eye contact or says a word.

"Fuck, what a body." The younger man turns to Marc with a maniacal smile, as if he expects him to be enjoying this as much as he is, then seems to remember who he is and shakes the gun at him like an accusatory finger. "Can't keep a slut that hot just for you, man. She needs to spread that shit around."

Brooke stares straight ahead.

Marc glares at him, wants to smash his face, to strangle him with his bare hands, but he can't seem to focus. A dull ache begins pulsating from the wound on his head and runs down along his jaw.

The other man orders Brooke to turn around and put her hands behind her back. She does as she's told. He pulls a plastic zip-tie from his back pocket and secures it tightly around her wrists.

They've done this before, Marc thinks. No one carries zip-ties around with them. They've come prepared for what is taking place, for what is about to happen. But who are they? And why are he and Brooke their victims? Chance, or was this planned? Have they been stalking them, preparing this for some time, waiting for the right moment when they could pounce? Have he and Brooke been targeted or are they simply unlucky enough to have come home right at the moment these men were in the area hunting prey?

As the man roughly spins Brooke back around so she is again facing them it hardly seems to matter. She's closed her eyes. Marc is sure she's begun to pray. He wishes he could too, but for some reason he can't remember any of the words.

"Now you," the older man says. "Get them clothes off."

Marc freezes, certain he's misunderstood. "What?"

In one quick move the big man places the point of his knife less than an inch from Brooke's face. "You want me to cut her?"

Woozily, Marc undoes his pants, lets them fall.

"Keep going, boy."

Fighting back a sudden wave of nausea, he pulls his underwear down as well. His skins flushes, the sensation spreading slowly throughout his entire body and mixing with the terrible tilting and whirling of the room.

The older man watches, his hand remarkably steady. In a way he's already dead, Marc thinks. There is nothing behind those eyes. No love, no compassion, sympathy or empathy, only sadistic hatred and a coldness that seems nearly impossible to imagine. He realizes then that he and Brooke are not even human to these men, not even animals. They're barely alive at all. They are unfeeling dolls, playthings with no real emotion, pain or fear. No one loves them and they love no one—not even each other—so it matters little if at all when they are tortured or killed. There is no meaning. They *have no meaning. They can do what they want and it won't matter, because none of them matter. And it has nothing to do with male or female, heterosexual or homosexual or even sex. Those things don't apply here. This is violence and cruelty as sport, as pastime, nothing more… but also nothing less.*

He lowers the knife. Throughout, Brooke's eyes have remained closed, but she comes back from her prayer as he nonchalantly cups one of her breasts, squeezes it then reaches around and cracks her ass with a violent slap. "Down on your knees, girl."

Face still expressionless, Brooke drops to her knees.

Fight back, Marc thinks, stop this. But he's so shaky he can barely stand.

The older man nods to his partner, who finally lowers the gun, and like an excited child, rushes over to Brooke. He gropes her violently then presses the gun to her forehead and unfastens his belt.

Pain arches through his head and the room bends again, but Marc takes a step toward them anyway. He falls, feet caught in the pants around his ankles.

"Get up, dumbass," the older man chuckles. "Get the fuck up."

Marc manages to regain his feet but all he can think about is the spinning game he used to play as a child, where he and his friends would twirl round and round then stop and try to walk. Just like then, the world is shifting and moving about crazily. He stumbles, not sure if he's fallen again, and then realizes he's still upright.

"Lay down across that face-first," he says to Marc, pointing to a loveseat on the opposite wall.

Marc shakes his head no.

"Make me tell you again," he says, raising the knife, "and I'll cut your wife's fucking throat before he can get his cock down it."

"You're going to cut it anyway," Marc says, the words gone from him before he can stop them. But they're not just words. They're truth, and they all know it. "You're going to kill us both no matter what we do or don't do."

"Even if you're right," he says, standing so close that Marc can smell his rancid breath, feel its warmth against his face. "You want me to fix it so you'll have to watch us kill her nice and slow?"

He looks to Brooke but she won't make eye contact. She stares straight ahead, as if in a trance, which he supposes, in a sense she is. His body shakes and he's sure he'll vomit, but he doesn't. Not yet.

The big man flashes a fist out quickly, slams it into

Marc's midsection. The blow doubles him over, knocks most of the air from him, and leaves Marc reeling. Before he's recovered, the man clutches the back of Marc's neck and shoves him toward the loveseat. Feet again tangled, he lurches forward, falling onto his hands and knees. He tries to stand but can't. His mind screams at him to fight and struggle, but his body is unable to respond.

Laughing, the shorter man slaps Brooke's face repeatedly with the head of his erection then adjusts his position so he can better reach her mouth.

From behind, a rough hand forces Marc forward until his face is buried in the cushions of the small sofa and he can no longer see anything.

Lord God, he thinks. How can this be happening?

As the older assailant moves in behind him and reaches around so he can place the knife blade against the side of his throat, Marc decides this man will be the first to die.

ಸಂಬ

Later, he remembers how the pain slaughtered disbelief. First came the repeated blows to the back of his head as he tried to get free, then the acidic nausea bubbled up, strangling him as he struggled to remain conscious and fight back. Wet, probing fingers, pressure, and finally, searing pain as the man stabbed into him. Sharp and brutal, it surged through him from the inside out, up along his spine and into the pit of his stomach, the back of his throat constricting as his body bucked in convulsive dry heaves, his mind a tempest of madness and chaos, the real and surreal exploding into one as hot breath pulsed against the back of his neck and saliva drizzled over his face in a long thick string, all of it set to rhythmic moans and guttural whispers until there was a violent and final shudder, and a warm spurting sensation deep in his rectum.

Several blurred and semiconscious memories follow… the horrible laughter of the other man… gagging sounds… slapping… and then he has somehow wound up on his back and Brooke, on all-fours, is dragged over to him by her hair and made to straddle him, her eyes wet, makeup smudged and eyeliner running along her cheeks in long narrow swathes like war paint, her nose bloodied, her flesh red. A pair of hands forces her face down between his legs, the men encouraging her, as if they've given her a choice…

And then… quiet… a strange silence in the house. It sounds so final.

And it is.

His entire body pulses with pain. It is the only thing that makes him think he may still be alive. His head feels odd… light and uneven and… and he can't think straight, not like he needs to, like he could before this began.

Vision returns soon after his hearing does, though it's distorted. He remains still, barely breathing, and waits until he's better able to focus. The shades are still drawn; he can see them from where he's laying on the floor. His eyes slowly pan the room; find Brooke laying a few feet away on her side, knees pulled up close to her chin. The plastic cord previously holding her hands behind her back has been cut away at some point, and although he can see her face, her eyes are closed. He wishes she'd open them. He needs her to open them. *Open your eyes, Brooke. Open them and let me know you're all right.*

She doesn't.

He looks beyond her. The younger man is collapsed on the loveseat, his pants in a heap next to him and his head back as if asleep. The gun is in one hand, resting against his thigh. His partner is not in the room, but Marc can hear rustling nearby. Is he in the kitchen, maybe?

This isn't over, he thinks. *They're just taking a break. They'll kill us. Eventually, when they've had their fill and done everything they want to do, they'll kill us both.*

He attempts to work his hands, his fingers. They clench into fists, release and clench again. He ever-so-slightly moves his feet and legs. Pain remains but its duller now, fading and becoming more of an ache. His mouth is dry as sand, and when he attempts a swallow he nearly chokes. Afraid the man may have heard him, he quickly shuts his eyes and feigns unconsciousness, but seconds later when he opens them he finds the man in the same position.

There are only two thoughts in his mind, repeating on an endless loop. One is his concern for Brooke. The other is his plan to murder both these men. Violence has come to their small town, their modest home, to his wife and himself. And now it will come to those who brought it.

Emotions fade. A merciless logic dominates his mind. His blood is cold.

He thinks a moment, the ideas and concepts coming to him a bit more easily now as he gradually recovers. *I need a weapon. Something, anything that will hurt this man enough so that I can get that gun from him...*

There, on the coffee table, about the size of his fist, a heavy glass paperweight...

He references useless information and memories on the origin of the paperweight, how it was a gift from his mother-in-law and how she'd purchased it while on vacation in Williamsburg, Virginia several years before. She'd had no idea that one day it might very well save the lives of her daughter and son-in-law. But perhaps someone—something—else did. Perhaps it was meant to be, intended all along for her to go into that particular artisan's shop, to buy that specific piece and for Brooke to decide to display it in their home precisely in that location, on a coffee table well within Marc's grasp.

"They got any beers in there?" the man asks without opening his eyes.

"Yeah," his partner answers from the kitchen.

Sated, the man on the loveseat absently scratches at his crotch and snuggles deeper into the cushions. "Bring me one."

"Hold on, I'm making a sandwich."

Marc realizes his pants were completely removed at some point. He sees them on the floor a few feet away in a tangled mess with his underwear. Again, he zeroes in on the man on the loveseat. His eyes have opened, but he's looking off in the direction of the kitchen, unaware that Marc is conscious.

"What kinda sandwich?"

In a single motion, Marc sits up and grabs the paperweight. Despite still feeling shaky and nauseous, he gets to his feet with remarkable ease then staggers forward. Just as the man seems to realize what's happening, Marc swings the paperweight down in an arcing motion hard as he can. He raises the gun but not in time, and the heavy piece of glass crashes the top of his head.

The paperweight bounces off his skull with a resounding clank, turning the warning he attempts into a muffled grunt. He appears stunned but not badly hurt, but sits there for a second, dazed and looking as if he's trying to figure out what just took place. At the same time Marc raises the paperweight and again brings it down onto his head, feeling the impact reverberate up into his wrist and arm.

This time the man slumps to the side and Marc closes on him, smashing the paperweight down across his head *again and again until the blood and perspiration between his fingers causes him to lose his grip. The paperweight finally falls free; rolls off the cushions then hits the floor with a dull thud.*

"Get in here," the man attempts to call out, but his voice is a slurred groan, and two thin lines of blood have already begun to leak from wounds high on his scalp, trickling down across his face like vines.

And then Marc's on him, pummeling the man with his fists, smashing his nose and mouth and grinding his knuckles into the man's eyes. As he topples over, Marc grabs for the gun.

Holding the man's gun-wrist with one hand, Marc cocks back the other and throws several more punches at the man's face. They connect with a sickening sound similar to a slap. The gun falls from his grasp and bounces away along the carpeted floor, but Marc continues striking him long after the man has slipped into unconsciousness. He hasn't hit another human being in years, not since high school. Until now he's never liked violence, has always found it abhorrent. But now he loves it, needs it, draws it into his body and absorbs it the way one inhales a wonderful breath of crisp fresh air. It feels...natural.

In what seems like hours but has only been a matter of seconds, Marc has disarmed and overpowered the man. As this realization dawns on him, he stops hitting him and steps back a moment. His hands are bloody, the skin along the knuckles split and bruised. He feels no pain.

"Shit, I can hear you from here," the older man says from the kitchen. "Hope that's not the bitch you're hitting like that. I ain't done with her yet don't bust her all up, asshole. Do the prick instead."

The sound of the man's voice stops him. Marc looks to the kitchen, his bare chest heaving. There is a clear line of sight from here to there, but the man is out of sight, probably sitting at the table.

He finds the gun and grabs it. It's much heavier than he anticipated.

The man on the loveseat moans.

Movement. Behind him.

Brooke is awake. Perhaps she has been throughout, he can't be sure. Still on her side, she's rolled over and facing him, her eyes wide. She nods slowly but emphatically, once and then again.

He answers with a nod of his own then turns and raises the gun, pointing it at the open doorway. The other man is coming. He can hear him.

"What the hell are you doing?" he asks as he crosses into the room, realizing too late that it's Marc he's talking to and not his partner. He freezes just inside the den, a half-eaten sandwich in one hand and the combat knife in the other. He's dressed but his pants are undone.

Their eyes meet and lock but neither man says a word.

"What the fuck you think you're gonna do with that?" he finally asks.

Marc shoots him.

The gun kicks and blood sprays from the man's neck as he falls back and collapses to the floor. He lay bleeding out on their carpet, violently twitching and trying to speak, his voice reduced to a gurgling rumble. The knife is still clutched in one hand, the bloody sandwich in the other.

The boom from the discharge is deafening in the small room, and Marc's ears ring to the point where he can no longer hear. He can smell the gun, feel the heat from it and the weight in his hand, but all sound is swallowed into a vacuum as he looks around frantically, focusing first on Brooke, who is now on hands and knees and crawling across the floor as if to get away, and then to the man on the loveseat, who has fought his way back toward something close to consciousness, and is attempting to stand.

He raises the gun and aims at the man on the loveseat, but doesn't fire. *No,* he thinks, *they'll hear. One shot might be ignored, missed or mistaken for something else. Two or more shots will not go unnoticed. They'll hear. And I don't want them to hear. Not yet.*

Marc places the gun on the coffee table, a safe enough distance from both men, then pries the knife from the older man's hand. Looking at the fingers, still curled as if holding the knife, Marc decides to snap a few. He breaks the man's index finger first, snapping it at the second knuckle. He's surprised the amount of force it takes, but once he knows the proper amount of pressure to apply he continues on and breaks the rest, pleased by the gasps of pain the man makes each time another bone cracks.

Once finished, with neither forethought nor hesitation, he turns and strides over to the loveseat and plunges the knife into the other man's thigh. He looks at it, buried there in the man's leg, as if it's the most fascinating thing he's ever seen. Perhaps it is. Marc yanks the blade free and thrusts it back into him once, twice, and then again.

It's so strange. It's not like movies, where things like this are always loud and histrionic. Instead it is almost sinfully quiet, only the grunting sounds and occasional soft cries from the man breaking the silence.

And he's not dead. Neither man is dead. Sometimes, he thinks, *people don't die quickly or easily. Sometimes they die slowly, sloppily.*

The man tries to get away but only manages to roll from the loveseat into a heap on the floor, grabbing at his wounds and moaning between sobbing cries, his face painted with pain and disbelief.

Marc stands above him. He can feel his heart smashing

his chest, his pulse pounding in his ears and temples. The man won't look at him. He wishes he'd look at him but he won't. Still, there is something oddly compelling here. And yet, it is callous and detached, his mind, body and soul transformed into a coldblooded reptilian version of the person he'd once believed himself to be.

"Motherfucker," the man gasps, "you, you—"

Marc stabs him again, this time in the back, just below his right shoulder, close to the neck. The man howls and tries to crawl away, so he stabs him again, deeper, and with more force. The blade snags on something—perhaps bone—and bends his wrist. He nearly drops the knife but tightens his grip just in time and pulls it free of the man's body.

Marc turns away as a ribbon of blood sprays his face. He realizes then that he's still nude. Expressionless and with mechanical movements, he finds his pants and pulls them on. Brooke has backed herself into the far corner of the room, knees drawn to her chin and eyes wide as saucers. Marc gathers her clothes, and without a word, places them on the floor next to her. Before he returns to the men, he touches her head, gently strokes her hair and the side of her face. He wants to smile but can't remember how. "Get dressed," he tells Brooke, his voice steady and calm. "Then call the police." She stares at him. "Brooke. Get dressed. Then call the police."

Trembling, she nods and begins to put her clothes on.

"Go on," he says once she's finished. "Use the phone in the kitchen."

She makes a move to hug him, to be hugged, but he stops her, holding his hand up like a traffic cop. He cannot feel. He cannot love. Not now.

"Call the police," he says again.

"What... what do I tell them?" she asks helplessly.

Marc looks at her. He has no idea. How do you explain

this?

"Are they dead?" she asks, voice still laced with shock.

The older man continues to gurgle and choke, drowning in his own blood, and his partner still tries to crawl away but is getting nowhere.

"Yes."

She nods knowingly, or perhaps he only remembers it that way.

"Don't come back in here," he says.

She doesn't.

Marc stands over the older man, watches him struggle to breathe a while, then squats down closer, placing the blade against the man's face. "Why did you come here?" he asks dully. "Why us? Who are you?"

The man attempts to respond but cannot speak in anything but an indecipherable gurgle. A burning pain pulses in Marc's anus and he clenches shut his eyes in an attempt to ward off the memories of this man on top of him. He grabs the man by the shoulder and rolls him onto his stomach. The man flops over like a ragdoll, the frightening and imposing figure he cast earlier barely a memory. Marc puts the knife beside him then pulls the man's pants down, tugging at them until they're around his knees. He retrieves the knife, leans in against the man and puts his mouth to his ear.

"Shhh," he whispers, mocking his attacker's earlier words, "it only hurts the first time."

He slams the blade and pulls it free, smashing it up and into him again and again until they're both slick with his blood and the man gurgles and spasms no more. Marc can feel the warm blood pumping from the man and running along his bare chest, arms and hands. And then a gut-wrenching smell rises, filling the room.

Marc rolls off him, leaving the knife buried in what remains of the man's mangled rectum, and turns his attention to his partner.

He has seen what happened and is trying desperately to get away, but he's lost too much blood, has too many wounds, and has nowhere to go.

"Don't," he pleads. "D-Don't!"

Marc crouches and studies him like a scientist considering a lab rat.

I can let you go... I don't have to kill you... if an ambulance gets here fast enough they could save you... you don't have to die...

But you will.

Marc climbs onto the man and pushes him back in a strange slow-motion maneuver. Easily pinning the wounded man to his back, he straddles his chest and places his hands around the man's throat. He looks into his eyes as he strangles him, never looking away even when the man's eyes have rolled to white and he bucks and vomits and writhes about in pools and puddles of blood and bile, urine and shit. Something leaves Marc in those empty violent moments, and something deep inside him breaks, shatters to pieces. Something he needs flees, and he knows even then it will never come back. It's not possible.

The man is dead. He continues to choke him a while anyway.

Finally, he climbs off, moves to the loveseat and sits down, back straight like he's waiting for a bus, bloody hands in his bloody lap.

Take their eyes, he thinks. *I should take their fucking eyes.*

By the time the police arrive he has succeeded.

☙❧

Blankets… he remembers they give them blankets. It's not cold but Brooke cannot stop shaking. He only knows the blanket one of the EMTs wraps around him is scratchy and weighs on his shoulders in a manner that causes him to want to shrug it off. There are a lot of people in their house, not just paramedics and police, but seven or eight men and a woman in suits, speaking quietly or with their hands over their mouths, milling about and taking notes, controlling things, organizing things, asking questions, listening, watching. They never speak directly to him (or Brooke), preferring instead to remain on the periphery. Only one man, an older bald man in khakis and an IZOD pullover who is clearly with them rather than the local police, speaks to them, and although he looks to be in charge he never introduces himself and Marc cannot remember anything he says.

It seems to happen so fast, this part. Everyone is there, vehicles and people and lights. And then, it's all gone. They're gone too, he and Brooke, strapped to gurneys and whisked away in the back of an ambulance. He remembers being only vaguely aware of the EMTs as Brooke reaches across the narrow gulf separating them and places one of her hands in his.

It is the most profound feeling of love he has ever felt.

They're taken to a hospital, but he doesn't recognize it. Or maybe the narcotics they've injected into his veins to stabilize and relax him have confused him. He can't be sure. He only knows he and Brooke are separated, and he's taken down a long and empty hallway to a dark room and left there on the gurney. *Why haven't they turned on the lights?* He wonders.

Marc is alone for a very long time, slipping in and out

of sleep.

"Marcus."

His eyes open.

"Marcus." *A voice from the darkness. Male, it sounds disembodied and artificial, like someone speaking through a voice-altering microphone perhaps.* "Can you hear me?"

He tries to speak but manages only a soft choking sound.

"You and your wife have been through a horrible ordeal, but the details surrounding this crime need not be released to the public. All anyone need know is that you and your wife were beaten and robbed at gunpoint by two escaped convicts, both of whom were ultimately killed when a struggle ensued during your efforts to defend yourself, your wife and your home. You're a hero, Marcus. It'll be in all the papers, on the local television stations."

"Am I dreaming?" *he asks; his throat so dry it hurts to speak.*

"Something similar," *the voice tells him.*

"Am I... alive?"

"Yes, Marcus, you're alive."

"Brooke..."

"She's being seen now. She's fine."

"Where am I?"

"You've been taken to a hospital. You've sustained some injuries, including a bad concussion, but physically, you're expected to make a full recovery. The rest... well, time will tell, won't it."

"Who are you?"

"Have you ever been stung by a bee, Marcus?"

"What?" *Head swimming, the darkness moves around him like ink.*

"A bee, Marcus, have you ever been stung by one?"

He tries to think. "Once... when I... when I was a

boy…"

"There was once a fascinating study conducted involving bee stings. Would you like to hear about it?"

He searches the darkness for the man but finds nothing, no one.

"The subjects weren't told ahead of time that bees were involved," the voice continues, "so the stinging came as a complete surprise and most subjects wrongly assumed a bee had simply gotten into the room by accident and stung them. Almost every subject reacted more or less the same when stung, regardless of personality or predisposed traits or beliefs. Even the most hardened pacifist among them, once stung, reacted by killing the bee. And many went beyond simply killing the creature. For many, the pain stirred in them something primeval. They swatted the bee, stomped it to dust, swore at it, and with few exceptions, killed it with furious anger. The bee had hurt them unexpectedly, and their response—in their fear and anger—was to not only kill it, but *completely* annihilate *it.*"

A tingling sensation behind Marc's eyes fans out across his face.

"That's what they want, Marcus. That's what they want to tap into, identify and extract from us. They want to produce a synthetic version that can be utilized at will, turned on and off like a switch."

"Who?" he asks, barely conscious now, his eyes closing despite his best efforts to keep them open.

"Just imagine the possibilities. We're a fascinating species with tremendous intellectual scope, capable of amazing acts of love, kindness, sacrifice. But we also possess the capacity for unthinkable violence and brutality. Luckily for you and your wife, Marcus, resilience in human beings is actually quite remarkable. We're not equipped with any sort of natural physical armor, save the skull, but even that's not ideal, in fact the manner in which we're designed leaves us extremely vulnerable physically. Instead, we have emotional and mental armor. For all our deficiencies and vulnerabilities in those areas as well, it's where our true armor resides. It's our saving grace in many ways, our downfall in others. Human beings can endure inconceivable amounts of emotional and mental devastation and often not only survive, but continue to function effectively. Of course there are mental hospitals full of people who never recover, but there are even more moving about in the world that have and continue to every day."

Something moves in the darkness… something small that scurries up over his elbow to his forearm, its tiny feet tickling his flesh. He wants to swat it away, wants it off him, but he can't move, the restraints hold him secure to the gurney, his arms pinned on either side of him.

"As Yeats wrote, 'All would be well could we but give us wholly to the dreams.' So true. Good luck to you, Marcus," the voice says. "Good luck to you."

But in that sad and lonely room, it is not the disembodied voice speaking to him from speakers hidden in the darkness he hears, it is something else…

And he understands. Even when his mind shreds, consumed by the impossible, his memories and thoughts, dreams and nightmares, fears and joys becoming one, swirling and falling about him like ash, a black, diseased, cancerous snow, he understands.

Shine…

The bee on his arm stings him, falls free and dies.

"Were you dreaming?" Doctor Berry asks, her legs crossed at the knee, one leg bobbing slightly.

"Am I dreaming now?"

She never answers. "Do you believe there was something more going on, Marc? Some sort of conspiracy, let's say?"

He watches her a while, trying to read her, but she exists in a language he doesn't speak. "I believe we were attacked by two escaped convicts."

"Do you believe that's all there was to it?"

"Shouldn't I?"

She gives a vague shrug. "It's not about should or shouldn't. It's about what you believe. What do you believe?"

"I believe I want to go home."

"Can you define that for me?"

He thinks about it a moment. "No."

"Do you think Brooke could if she were here?"

"I think Brooke would say something like she doesn't have the luxury of shutting down."

"But you do?"

"I haven't shut down. I've awakened."

Doctor Berry arches an eyebrow. "What have you awakened to?"

He closes his eyes, remembers the last time he was home with Brooke, and how they'd spent hours sitting together, saying nothing, watching the world through the windows of the living room. Winter was setting in.

"In nature, animals mask injuries to survive and stay safe," she'd said, her voice a hollow echo in the empty house.

"You're not in the jungle, Brooke."

"I'm not?"

"They made you suck their cocks."

She brought a hand to her face, rubbed her eyes. "Why do you say these things to me? Why do you say them *so nasty and mean and dirty? You just blurt them out as if they have no meaning. They raped me, Marc, the same as you."*

"No," he reminded her, "not the same as me."

Silence again enveloped the room. Marc strode to the window facing the street. The same unmarked car with tinted windows that had been there on and off for days was parked a ways down on the opposite side of the road. "Why are they out there?" *he asked.* "Why are they watching us? We're the victims."

"Maybe they're afraid."

"Afraid of what?"

"Of you."

He looked back over his shoulder at her.

"Of what you might do," *she added.* "Aren't you? Aren't you afraid of what you might do?"

"Not anymore."

"Marc?" Doctor Berry's voice opens his eyes, returns him to her cramped office. Someone groans then screams out from a nearby hallway, but such sounds are so commonplace here he scarcely notices them anymore. "Marc, what have you awakened to?"

Tears well in his eyes, spill free. He can still feel the man inside him; still feel his warm blood dripping through his fingers; still remember the sounds of their final dying breaths. "God," he says softly. "I think it's God."

Thirteen

Sparse candlelight barely illuminating the way, Marc shuffles behind Sister Sarah as she makes her way through winding catacombs beneath the farmhouse. An old and musty odor hanging in the air fills his nostrils, along with the earthy aroma of dirt and decay. The only sounds are their muted footfalls and the swishing fabric of Sarah's habit as it moves with each step she takes. Shadows bend and creep along the tunnel walls, and Marc does his best to ignore the horribly oppressive and claustrophobic feeling closing around him, mindful that he is deep underground, an ant negotiating dark and narrow passageways carved into the earth by others who came well before him yet knew even then that they were preparing the way for those to come.

You've chosen this path, Marcus. It belongs to you.

Perhaps the claustrophobic feel of the corridors is to blame, or the lack of decent air, but Marc feels lightheaded and then rather suddenly drowsy, as if he's ingested a sedative his system is struggling to fight off. He reaches out and touches the wall to his right, steadying himself as he follows along after Sarah, her dark robes blurring and leaving trails as they move about her.

They come to a section where another corridor bends to their left, but Sarah continues straight ahead, never slowing.

As Marc turns to look down the adjacent passageway, he sees light. Not fire, *light.* He stops, leans against the wall and draws some deep breaths. Unaware of his respite, Sarah keeps on.

"Sarah," he says. "Wait!"

Movement within the light catches his eye. At the end of the corridor is a room of some kind. Thick red curtains of velvet hang across the doorway, but stand open. There are people in the room—women—all women—sitting or lying around on velvet couches and chairs, some standing and talking quietly amongst themselves, drinks in their hands, cigarettes between their lips, others smoking drugs from small glass or metal pipes. The women are all heavily made up and dressed in flimsy pieces of lingerie, like prostitutes in a brothel waiting on the next wave of johns. At their feet, the floor is alive, crawling and slithering, a blanket of insects and snakes tangled together and flopping about.

As Marc moves deeper into the passage, a beautiful woman in a bustier, satin panties and spike heels notices him and rises from a couch. *The night nurse*, he realizes. *Skuld... the future.* Only now her hair is fire red, piled atop her head and held in place with ornate sticks. She grabs the curtains on either side of the doorway, and with a decidedly demonic glare, angrily yanks them shut.

From behind the curtain comes a series of loud clicks, then horrible tearing sounds echo through the catacombs followed by a shrieking cry and a violent intake of breath.

"*Yes,*" a voice hisses.

Marc turns and staggers back into the main passageway. Sister Sarah is gone. There is only darkness now. He calls out for her, his voice hollow in the blackness. "Sarah, where are you?" Feeling the sides of the catacombs as he goes, he shuffles in the direction she'd been leading him. Taking each step carefully, he strains to see through the darkness ahead but cannot be sure of anything. Without the luxury of candlelight he quickly becomes disoriented.

In the distance he hears what sounds like running water. Rain?

Through the darkness, a flicker of light...

He moves toward it, quickening his pace, but soon realizes it is not Sister Sarah's candle but another, a series of them in fact, their flames bending into the main corridor from another side-room. Marc leans to the wall again, and peers down the tunnel to his right.

The room looks to be a small underground chapel of sorts, and there is something cast on the wall, something enormous.

The shadow of a cross, upside down...

A group of impossibly old nuns in black habits are knelt in prayer, pale, bloodless, ravaged faces turned to the inverted cross above them, their hushed mantras drifting through the catacombs in a droning rumble. Religious artifacts from every conceivable religion are scattered about the chapel, on the floor, on tables, even the walls. Odd books showcasing ancient drawings and texts lay open near a bank of candles burning on the far side of the room. Yet rainwater leaks from the ceiling, pours down from the world above, caught by various ornate goblets and ceremonial bowls.

Growling whispers murmur, emanate from some deeper part of the room Marc cannot see from his position. Rather than investigate its source he moves away as quietly as he can, again following the walls of the main corridor.

Forcing away thoughts that he could be trapped in these catacombs forever, he follows the contours of the walls through the thick darkness until he hears something familiar, the faint swishing sound of Sister Sarah's habit. But there is no sign of her candle. He advances, slowly, quietly.

A strange red hue cuts the darkness, seeping through

it and casting the area with the look of a colored filter placed over a camera lens. At the farthest reaches of light, he sees a nun standing in the main corridor, her back to him.

"Sarah?" he asks in a loud whisper.

She looks over her shoulder with her bright green eyes and gives a subtle nod. It is then that he sees she still has her flame, but is cupping it with her hand. Marc sidles up next to her then follows her gaze to something at the end of a long hallway.

The red light originates from behind a sheer curtain, casting whatever is behind it in silhouette. It takes a moment for his eyes to adjust, but once they have he sees the shape of someone lying on a bed behind the curtain, nuns positioned around the bed in a semi-circle, heads bowed. The prone figure stirs a bit, and a groan wafts into the catacombs. It doesn't sound entirely human, and as Marc continues to watch he realizes the silhouette on the bed isn't either.

The red shadow is clearly female but as it changes positions an appendage behind it sways and bends in the air, long and oddly graceful.

Like a tail, Marc thinks.

He instinctually takes a step back as the panic of terror sets in.

"Shhh," Sarah whispers, a finger to her lips. "The Devil's back there."

"It's another of them, isn't it?"

"*Urd*," she says. "Fate... the past... those are her domains. Together with her sisters they control it all, the past, the present, the future. But like the others, and like *Yggdrasil*—like all of us, really—she's dying."

When he returns his gaze to the curtain the silhouette has changed and more closely resembles the crippled old woman he encountered at the church in the forest. "The third sister... *Verdandi*... the present..."

"You've not yet seen her. But she's here." As Sarah moves away down the main corridor, he follows, determined to not be distracted again by whatever else resides within this bad dream of his, sealed off in these long-forgotten tombs.

Eventually they stop and Sarah shines her candle on a closed door. "The catacombs are deeper and more extensive than you can even begin to imagine," she tells him. With her free hand she pulls open the door. It scrapes a bit but gives way easily. Beyond the door lies an enormous stone staircase leading up to a distant pinpoint of light. "But this will lead you closer to the way out. This will lead you up."

"To Brooke and Spaulding?"

She nods. "Eventually."

"Show me, take me to them. You said you'd take me to them."

"This is far as I can go. This is your path. It belongs to you."

"But you brought me down here."

"As they instructed," she tells him, looking nervously behind her at the darkness from which they've come. "Go now. Hurry, please hurry."

"What's waiting for me up there, Sarah?"

Candlelight flickers across her face, the shadows distorting her beauty, or perhaps hinting at what truly lies beneath it. "Set us free, Victim Soul," she whispers, backing away into darkness. "*All* of us. Set us free."

He looks to the steps and then back to Sister Sarah, but she's gone, one with the darkness now.

Marc begins his ascent.

"What else do you remember, Marc? Can you tell me?"

"I'm trying," he assures Doctor Berry. *"I know there's more but..."*

The air in her office is thick, oppressive. She seems unfazed by it. *"You said you felt as though you'd awakened to God,"* she reminds him in her soothing voice.

He paws the tears away, feeling stupid and vulnerable in his little chair in her little office. *"I don't know, I..."*

"Let's explore that." She brings a hand to her face, lets the tip of her index finger rest in the corner of her mouth. *"Did you have a particularly religious upbringing?"*

"I was raised Catholic," he explains. *"But we weren't fanatics or anything."*

"So then, for you, this would all have a decidedly Christian bent."

"Not necessarily. I mean, I am a Christian, I suppose, but..."

"But?"

"But I don't believe like I used to, not across the board anyway. For the most part I think we're all wrong."

"No one's right then?"

"God is right. Man is wrong."

"Understood, but if we were to refer to a religious text that you had some experience with, as a Christian it would be the Bible, yes?"

"I read it years ago as a child and young adult but not since."

"And what did you think?"

"I don't believe it literally, and much of it I find ridiculous and distasteful." He shrugs with indifference. *"But like anything else, there's good and bad in it."*

"Wouldn't it make sense for God to reach us through whatever vehicle we know and are familiar with? For you, it would be a Christian-based approach because that's what

you know and were raised with."

"Yes, but as an adult I haven't had much use for religion of any kind."

"Yet you believe in God."

"I do. I just think it's much deeper than any of us understand, greater than any old books or stories, far more complex and personal than that. But, yes, in some form I believe there's a God, a greater power, whatever you want to call it."

"What do you want to call it?"

"I call it God."

Dr. Berry uncrosses her legs and readjusts her position. "All right then, if God exists, is there total separation between God and Man or do you believe a bridge exists between the two?"

"I believe there's a bridge."

"Following that thought, there's often a lot of talk about bringing people to God, yes? But what about bringing God to people? How do you do that? What connects God to people?"

After brief contemplation he says, "Creation."

"Good," she replies, eyes wide. "See that through to the end."

"Without creation there can be no God. A god can't be a god until it's worshipped, revered, feared or even questioned, believed in or not believed in. Without creation none of that's possible because there's no one else there to have those thoughts or feelings. Without its creations it would exist alone in a void, not yet a god."

"So," Dr. Berry says, flashing a bright smile, "until a god brings forth its creations, it cannot truly be a god."

"No creation, no god."

"Logically, wouldn't this be a cyclical concept?"

"Yes."

"*No god, no creation either.*"

He nods. "*A god without creation is not a god. And there can be no creation without a god.*"

"*What about science, Marc?*"

"*Science is also a god.*"

"*And those who don't believe in gods at all?*"

"*Their belief—or disbelief—is their god.*"

"*So would you say that without gods we don't exist?*"

"*One cannot exist without the other. We need each other. The question is, did God create us, or did we create God?*"

"*Which do you believe?*"

"*I don't think it matters.*"

"*Do you think God has chosen you, Marc?*"

Discomfort stirs in the pit of his stomach. "*I don't know.*"

"*If he has, for what purpose exactly, do you know? Surely there would have to be a purpose, no?*"

Set us free, Victim Soul…

"*Yes. I just…*" *Pain flares through his temple. He touches it with his fingertips. His flesh is warm and clammy.*

"*If there is a God then there must be some reason for you to have been put through such an incomprehensible amount of misery and hardship,*" *she says.* "*Or is it all random, a cosmic coincidence of some sort?*"

All of us.

"*I miss my wife,*" *he says softly, the words catching in his throat.* "*I miss her, I—I miss us. And I want it back.*"

Set us free.

Dr. Berry lets him sit with his thoughts a while. After a few moments she says, "*Maybe we should discuss the accident. I think you're ready.*"

He stares at her, confused. "*The accident?*"

"*The car accident, Marc.*"

Something inside him begins to thrash and fight, violently struggling to break free, to run from all that is slowly closing in on him. Wolves, he thinks, a pack of wolves creeping, circling, gradually closing the distance, closer and closer, jaws snapping and drooling in anticipation, eager to tear him to pieces.

"The car accident in upstate New York," she presses, raising her eyes to meet his. "The car accident that took the lives of your wife and best friend."

Fourteen

In the narrow space, Marc's screams of rage and agony echo below him, as if they've come from someone else. Mind splintering, he forces himself up the steps. But for the pinpoint of light in the distance, darkness reigns, and though he climbs hard and fast as he can, the light remains the same size and intensity. Heart drumming his chest and eyes straining to see, he continues a bit further, ignoring the musty odor permeating the area. "Take me," he tells the light. "That's what you want." Stopping, he falls against the wall and tries to catch his breath. *I'm the one you want, the one you need. Take me and give Brooke the life I saw in dreams: the life with Spaulding in the cabin in the woods, she was happy there. Give it to her.* "This is her dream. Wake her up and take me."

Somewhere nearby he can hear water running, surging, strong and violent and alive. Countless thoughts and visions fill his head, firing one into the next to form an endless montage. Brooke, Spaulding, the men in the driveway, the three sisters, the strange nuns, the shadow of an inverted cross creeping across the wall, the church in the woods, the strange forest runners, Wilma in her cottage, the catacombs, the deer darting before the car, the sounds of impact, the whispers and growls, fire and water, blood and bone, death and life, love and hate, violence and peace, chaos and serenity, all of it rolling over and engulfing him in a relentlessly suffocating fog.

In the distance the light still beckons.

Whispers everywhere… circling him… stalking him … until one breaks free… a woman's voice from somewhere not so very far away. Her words drift past but she remains concealed in darkness, hidden in the impossible…

"… 'And he dreamed that there was a ladder set up on the earth, and the top of it reached to heaven; and behold, the angels of God were ascending and descending on it'…"

Marc looks behind him. "Sarah?"

The stairs vanish into deeper darkness, divulging nothing. Above him, the light burns on. But is it salvation or simply a dying star, the failing light of what little remains, of what once was; the last bit of life, of him?

Set us free, Victim Soul.

Marc chases the light and all that resides behind and within it, aware now of what must happen, and what he must do to make it so.

Below, more screams echo forth. They are not his own.

ಸಿಂಧ

Rain falls across the farmhouse. A soft and quiet rain, a trick, an ambush as the storm bides its time, waits for the moment it can regain power and strike with merciless anger.

As it must… as it was created to do…

Creasing the darkness, the ancient tree stands alone on the horizon, its thick trunk and gnarled branches slowly transforming from a blackened and burned appearance to a more ethereal shade of gray.

Gardens of Night

Below, the wells, the farmhouse, the sisters…

The past… the present… the future…

Three wooden wells with draw buckets not far from the tree catch the rain, bad dreams of the living, the dead, the damned, the enlightened and the insane, dark fairytales, mythology, evil government conspiracies and the prophecies of Messianic martyrs and killers alike.

Flames slash night.

From the farmhouse come the twelve nuns. Carrying enormous burning torches, they walk in single file across the lot toward the tree, the wells; their destinies.

The darkness around them burns.

The brilliance of the fire, along with the heat, stirs the old man in the outbuilding. He staggers out, sees the others then looks to the night sky as if for answers. Continuing their slow walk up the side of the hill to Yggdrasil, the nuns pay him no attention, and he hurries to the farmhouse and disappears inside.

Somewhere far off, thunder rumbles.

ଛଠ

The higher Marc climbs, the narrower the passage and the lower the ceiling becomes, boxing him in and causing him to crouch, and then crawl the remainder of the way, taking the stairs on hands and knees. Exhausted, he pushes forward on his stomach, feeling claustrophobic in what has become such a cramped and confined space, his already injured hands scraping the rock walls on either side of him, his scalp brushing the coarse ceiling above him. The light is brighter but still small. He finally reaches the top of the stairs and the small wooden door that resides there. A trapdoor? He wonders. Maneuvering closer, he realizes the light is leaking through an inordinately large keyhole slightly bigger than a fifty-cent piece. The beam is littered with particles of rock-dust, dirt and debris floating through it in a slow spiral, and he can smell fresh, vibrant air just beyond the door. He struggles to get closer in the hopes of getting the door open or at a minimum peeking out through the hole to whatever lies on the other side, but when he's mere inches away the light grows significantly dimmer.

An eye appears in the opening, bloodshot… unblinking… subhuman.

Marc wriggles back and away from it, attempting to hide in the darkness as groans and growls fill the musty air. But suddenly as the eye appears, it darts away, returning the beam to the stairway.

The door begins to rattle… softly at first, then violently. Whatever it is tries to get in but is unable to do so. It screams as if wounded and shuffles away.

Marc lies still a while, breathing heavily and trying to remain calm while wedged into the tomblike stairwell. The light remains uninterrupted for several minutes. He fears going through the door but knows he has no choice. He cannot stay here, he either had to get out or turn around and go all the way back to the bottom and hope Sarah didn't lock that door behind him.

Sisyphus chasing after his boulder…

Crawling forward, he props himself up on one elbow and, ignoring the pain, slams his already damaged palm against the door. It refuses to move. He tries again, and again. The door won't budge.

And then he hears it again. Water. Surging, rushing…

It begins to run beneath the door, trickling at first, then coming faster and faster still, spraying cold and violently through the keyhole and flooding the stairs with startling power. Marc tries to turn away but can't. The passage has become far too narrow for him to change positions. His only choice is to back down the steps blind, feet-first.

As the cold water crashes his face, he drops his head, tucks chin to chest and attempts a deep breath.

His lips taste like salt.

❧☙

A wall of fire cuts the night sky. The nuns, their flaming torches hoisted high, stand at the summit of the hill, six to one side of Yggdrasil, six to the other.

Through the crackle of fire and the soft rain, their voices rise in unison, reciting a passage from the *Völuspá* that will call forth their mistresses.

"*Thence comes the maidens… mighty in wisdom… three from the dwelling down 'neath the tree…*"

The front door to the aged farmhouse opens with a sinister creak.

"*Urth is one named…*"

A shadow figure emerges, its body covered from head to toe in what appears to be a dark shroud of some kind.

"*Verthandi the next—on the wood they scored—and Skuld the third…*"

Two more follow in single file, each holding a burning candle as they move across the farm toward the hill.

"*Laws they made there, and life allotted to the sons of men…*"

The shrouds brush the ground and conceal their feet. They could be walking or gliding, floating just above the ground, it is impossible to know for sure.

"*…and set their fates…*"

As the Three Fates reach the top of the hill, the nuns start back toward the farmhouse, their torches lighting the way. The last in line touches her fire to a bush near Yggdrasil and it bursts into flame, illuminating the otherwise dark hill even after the nuns have returned to night, their torches extinguished suddenly and without explanation, as if they'd never truly been there at all.

At the edge of the field on the other side of the hill, a fox, watching the proceedings since they began, slips away into the trees. He does not go unnoticed.

ಸಿಂಧ

The water continues to rush free, crashing over him and flooding the stairway. Marc struggles back to his hands and knees and reaches for the door again, but the force of the water makes it impossible now, and he slumps back, submitting to its strength, certain it will wash him away and back down the stairs to the darkness below.

But just as he prepares to be carried off, the door splits and implodes under the force with a loud crack. Shards of wood fall about him, carried off in the frenzy of water, the beam replaced with a shaft of light instead, a sanctuary of warm and bright light unlike anything he's seen before.

Shine...

And for the first time, he understands.

Fighting desperately, Marc throws a hand up toward the opening, grabs hold of the side and attempts to pull himself up. But the water just keeps coming, and he soon loses his grip and flops back to the stairs, impossible amounts of seawater blasting through the opening now, taking him under, sliding him back down the stairs, blocking the beautiful light and all else as he holds his breath and feels his body slipping away on the current. Clenching shut his eyes, he's pulled down into the cold water, swallowed in an ocean of water pouring over him and sucking him down into the endless darkness of the catacombs.

But in the deafening rush, all he sees, all he knows is Brooke.

ഩൢ

From the first well, the hag Urd draws her bucket while her sisters look on. With aged but deft hands she carries the full bucket to Yggdrasil and pours the water at the base of the tree, at the root, watching as the ground absorbs it. After replacing the bucket to the well, Urd peels back her hood and looks to Yggdrasil with cataract-covered eyes. Moonlight and flames from the nearby bush conspire to illuminate her face, and within moments of emptying her bucket, Yggdrasil looks healthier, and although still an old woman, Urd becomes decidedly younger. Miraculously, her eyes clear and the cataracts burn away as she mutters quiet prayers.

ഩൢ

Twisting, turning, submerged and struggling to draw breath, Marc fights and thrashes against the onslaught as he falls lower and lower, sucked down as if into a great drain, or the gaping mouth of some gargantuan creature.

Water is passage...

He hears screams but they're in his head, tearing at him like something trapped within his skull clawing desperately to get out.

And then everything goes dark and the world sleeps.

※

Skuld steps forward, raises her arms. "*Mimir*, protector of this well and water spirit of great wisdom, we thank you." She draws a bucket, pours it across the lower branches of Yggdrasil then removes her hood. Clearly the youngest, even in limited light she is voluptuous, erotic and beautiful as ever.

Once she has finished her prayers and again conceals herself beneath the hood, the third sister approaches the final well.

She is met by a strong gust of wind. Night, whispering secrets of what is yet to come…

※

It is not water, but fire he steps through, effortlessly moving between the flames and at one with the inferno from which he comes. Unharmed, he steps onto a rural dirt road and walks toward a small cabin in the distance. He knows this place. Like so much else, he has dreamt it.

It is early morning.

He can hear birds singing, but not just singing, *communicating*, leading him closer to where he must go.

Like a fever dream, everything is slightly blurred and

vaguely out of synch.
Don't let them fool you...
He stops, closes his eyes.
Not birds—Archie—his roommate at the mental hospital.
Chemical Apocalypse, that's all it is, see?
The corpulent middle-aged former electrical engineer, scribbling in his ever-present notebook, manically running a hand over his bald head, lips moving, working various scenarios and equations, sits on the edge of his bed. Now and then he glances over at Marc as if to be sure he's still there, or perhaps because he suspects he may not be there at all.
It's all a test, an experiment gone wrong.
"No," Marc says. "It's more than that."

ಬಿಂ

Considerably broader and taller than her sisters, Verdandi removes her hood to reveal a young woman with a pretty but stern face. She looks to the well, Yggdrasil, and the distant forest beyond.

The large gray serpent, until then camouflaged in the tree, slithers to higher branches, its black eyes locked on the sisters even when four deer emerge from the dark field below and stride to the top of the hill. They stop, acknowledge the sisters then lope off in different directions.

"The four winds," Verdandi whispers, "scatter to the corners of the Earth."

Marc opens his eyes, banishes Archie and the hospital to darkness, and focuses instead on the cabin. There's a pickup and a small SUV in the driveway, both relatively new, and though the cabin is modest it is well kept and situated on a beautiful plot of land set between two rolling green hills, a field of flowers to the front of the house, a large expanse of forest to the rear.

He continues down the dirt road then stops suddenly.

Spaulding stands on the front porch of the cabin. Although his face bore a few scars he never used to have, he looks vibrant and clear-eyed, healthier, happier, younger and content with himself. In one hand he holds a cigarette, the other he raises to his forehead to shield his eyes as he scans the field of flowers.

And then Marc sees what his old friend is searching for.

There, in the field, walking gracefully toward the cabin… Brooke. A small black puppy runs by her side.

Spaulding waves with a big, exaggerated, arcing motion. It achieves what he'd hoped for, and catches her attention. She waves back, though far more subtly, brushes a wisp of hair from her face and squints up at the sun.

She is the most beautiful vision Marc has ever seen.

Brooke is alive. Happy. Safe.

He sees Spaulding smile wide then take a long drag on his cigarette.

Brooke picks up the puppy, snuggles him, and with a wonderfully carefree laugh he hasn't heard from her in years, continues on with the dog under her arm.

Marc calls out to her, quickening his pace along the dirt road. Determined to get to Brooke before she reaches the cabin he breaks into a run, kicking up dirt as he goes and continuing to call Brooke's name even though it's clear neither she nor Spaulding can hear him. He reaches the field of flowers and bounds across it, closing on her. "Wait!" he screams. "Brooke, wait!"

He is within a few feet of her but still running hard when he reaches out to touch her hair. His fingertips brush the back of her head, gently caress her, and she stops and looks back over her shoulder, startled.

But she cannot see him.

Pain stabs Marc's chest like a dagger, and he draws a sudden and violent breath, as if he hasn't taken one in some time. Or as if it's the last breath he'll ever know. His throat constricts and his body seizures uncontrollably.

He knows... he *knows*... but had hoped they'd grant him more time.

Lack of oxygen drops him to his knees, and as he falls over, gagging on an explosion of blood firing up into his throat, the last thing he sees is Brooke gazing out at the field behind her, a puzzled look on her face.

※※

Verdandi draws her bucket. When it reaches the top of the well, her eyes roll to white and she throws back her head, plunging her hands into the water with an orgasmic moan. "Blood of the martyr... Victim Soul... set us free."

She pulls her hands free. They come back slick with bright red blood. Grasping the bucket carefully, she pours the mixture of well water and blood across several of Yggdrasil's higher branches.

"*Surt,*" she whispers, "giant of Muspelheim, remain in

your realm of fire... *Ragnarok,* doom of the gods... *Gotterdammerung,* end of the universe no more. Yggdrasil lives."

Moments later, hood in place, she rejoins her sisters as Yggdrasil begins to change, the branches growing healthier and stronger.

Behind them, the farmhouse erupts into fire.

Watching from the front window, her wooden cross clutched in her hands, Sarah closes her eyes, smiles and begins to pray, ignoring the flames even as the old building burns and collapses down upon her.

ఞ⚮

"My wife is alive," he tells her. "She and Spaulding survived the accident."

Dr. Berry's face remains expressionless, and for a while she says nothing, as if expecting him to continue. All he knows is that he has to get out of this place, away from here, away from all of this.

"And what about you, Marc?" she finally asks.

"What about me?"

"Did you survive the accident?"

He looks to the lone window in the office, a crisscross of security wire sandwiched between two thick panes of glass. Rain sluices along the window, blurring the dreary parking lot beyond. Does it ever stop raining here? He wonders. "No," he says softly. "I didn't."

Fifteen

Black ash falls from a gray sky, gracefully descending to Earth. It doesn't accumulate, disintegrating the moment it lands, but leaves the world a strangely magical dreamscape.

Alone in the rec room, Marc watches the black snow through the windows. The hospital is unusually quiet, stranding him in indecisive silence. While the meds have left him calm and even, they cannot mute those things only he can hear.

"Do you hear the whales again?"

He turns from the windows, sees Dr. Berry standing in the doorway and nods. "I hear them while I'm awake now."

In one of her business suits and heels, briefcase in hand, she looks professional-chic and attractive as ever. He wonders how old she is. More or less his age probably, but it's hard to tell. "Are they talking to you?" she asks.

"Yes."

"What are they saying?"

"Before, I thought they were asking for deliverance."

"And now?"

"I realize they're offering it."

She smiles with her dark eyes. "The voice of God?"

"I hope so."

"Maybe it's the universe calling you back to where you

began, where we all begin. Maybe there are countless voices within that realm most can't hear. But you can. You hear them; those voices that were always there and always will be, flooding your mind, overwhelming and frightening, enlightening, oddly comforting and confusing all at once."

Marc slowly closes the gap between them until only a few feet separate them. "You've known all along, haven't you?"

Unexpectedly, she reaches out with her free hand and cups the side of his face. Her palm is soft and warm. "Doesn't matter," she says, and with a wink, turns and walks away down the dark corridor leading to the exit, her heels clicking against the floor as she goes.

Marc wants to stop her but knows he can't.

Partially concealed in shadow, she stops at a pair of heavy double doors at the end of the hallway. "Just remember," Dr. Berry says without looking back, "the glory's not in death, Marc. Never has been. The glory's in life. It's always been in life."

She pushes open the doors and walks through into the slowly dying afternoon. One door gradually closes behind her.

The other remains open.

Marc starts down the corridor, slowing only as he passes his old room and notices Archie sitting on his bed scribbling madly in his tattered notebook. Their eyes meet. Archie forms a gun with his fingers, points it at his temple and pulls the trigger, silent but grinning throughout.

༄༅

Gardens of Night

Through the falling ash, Marc walks across the empty parking lot. No one tries to stop him. Beyond the lot he finds tall grass swaying gently in the breeze. He smells the ocean. It's close.

Grass becomes dunes. He climbs up, struggling for purchase in the shifting sand, past the overturned and rotting carcass of a familiar automobile, and continues to the summit, where he gazes down across a long stretch of empty beach and placid ocean beyond. The wind catches his hair and face, and he breathes it in deeply, filling his lungs. He looks back at the car only once more, studies it for a time then proceeds down the side of the dune to the beach below.

As he stands near the shoreline, waves lapping his feet, Marc undresses, remembering these very winds blowing in off the Atlantic while lying in bed with Brooke on summer nights. Soft, hot wind, as he remembers, blowing gently through their bedroom, disturbing delicate chimes she'd hung just outside the window near their bed. He remembers awakening to the winds and the ethereal chime-songs, and watching Brooke sleep, curled up on her side, knees drawn in tight. Before the whales... before the blood... and yet in this moment it all seems so close, forged together into a single entity, a long and winding thread running through the remnants of a thoroughly shattered life, which of course it is.

He looks back over his shoulder at the dunes. Three figures in shrouded hoods stand watching. The first looks to the left, the second faces him and the third looks to the right... Urd to the past, Verdandi to the present, Skuld to the future.

He blinks and they're gone.

Marc slowly walks into the surf. Despite how cold and gripping the water is, once it reaches his calves he dives through an incoming wave and swims to deeper water.

Guide me gently...

He breaks the surface, draws breath and bobs along the waves, letting the sea carry him away. Arms making slow arcing motions to cut the water and legs treading beneath, he looks to the gray sky and the setting sun.

Darkness is coming, night eternal. But he feels neither pain nor fear.

Not anymore. Not ever again.

...softly over to Thy Kingdom shore...

Marc closes his eyes and lets the ocean take him, forcing himself beneath the surface, spiraling down into another kind of darkness, one he embraces even as his muscles grow tired, his body weakens and his lungs ache and burn for oxygen that will never arrive.

If Brooke were with me, she'd hold my hand and we'd cling to each other. Looking into each other's eyes, we'd let the sea take us. Together. And nothing else would matter. Only this moment... only us... safe in each other's love.

But not this time, my love...

Submerged, the ocean is below, above and all around him.

But he is not alone. The whales have not abandoned him after all.

Speak to me... tell me your secrets... whisper them in my ear...

Fairytales... myths... real as the darkest woods, the deepest oceans, the most immense skies and profound as the greatest love, the utmost evil, and the ultimate sacrifice...

He remembers Brooke as he always will now, a smart, beautiful, special woman, his partner, lover and best friend, holding a puppy and looking out across the field of flowers from which she'd come, a look of confusion and, oddly, peace etched across her face as she tries to understand how she could've just felt him there, running his fingers through her hair and whispering to her as he so often did when they'd held each other tight. And then she's smiling in the glow of those memories. Gone from him…but not so very far…

Free me, he tells the whales. *Heal me.*

And as their melancholy songs draw him closer and closer to gardens unseen, where horrors of the past hold no power and fate is not a hammer but an embrace, a kiss, the hand of one you love holding tight to your own, they do.

ACKNOWLEDGEMENTS

Thank you to Robert Dunbar, Chas Hendricksen and everyone involved with **UNINVITED BOOKS**. I'm honored to have my work involved in the launch of such an exciting and important new independent publishing company. Thanks also to my wife Carol, and to all my family and friends. And as always, thank you to the readers and fans all over the world for their continued loyalty and support.

ABOUT THE AUTHOR

The son of teachers, Greg F. Gifune was educated in Boston and has lived in various places, including New York City and Peru. A trained actor and broadcaster, he has appeared in various stage productions and has worked in radio and television as both an on-air talent and a producer. Earlier in life he held a wide range of jobs, encompassing everything from journalism to promotions. An acclaimed, respected editor, he served as Editor-in-Chief of *Thievin' Kitty Publications*, publishers of the magazine *THE EDGE, Tales of Suspense* and currently serves as Associate Editor at *Delirium Books*. The author of numerous novels, screenplays and two short story collections, his work has been consistently praised by critics and readers alike, and has been translated into several languages and published all over the world. Greg and his wife Carol live in Massachusetts with a bevy of cats. Discover more about his writing at www.GregFGifune.com.

Also from Uninvited Books

SHADOWS
Supernatural Tales by Masters of Modern Literature

With an introduction by Robert Dunbar, this collection features terrifying explorations of the unknown by D. H. Lawrence, Virginia Woolf, E. M. Forster, Edith Wharton, Henry James, Willa Cather and many of the other great writers who revolutionized dark fiction.

In paperback

> Between the idea
> And the reality
> Between the motion
> And the act
> Falls the Shadow.
> ~ *T. S. Eliot*

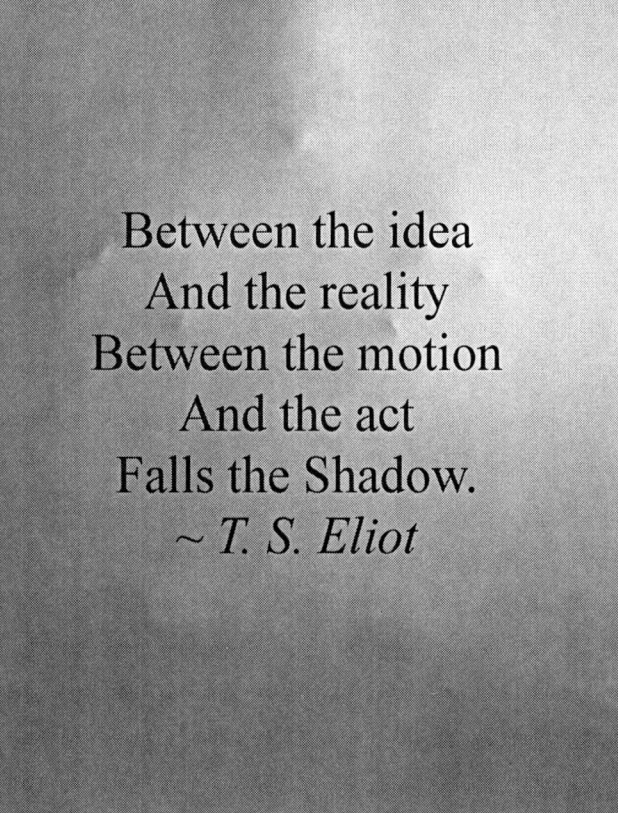

UNINVITED BOOKS

ILLUMINATING DARKNESS

UNINVITED BOOKS is an independent press dedicated to restoring the mantle of literary distinction to dark fiction.

UninvitedBooks.com